Inhalt

W0346461

Sobald die Lösungen der Original-Prüfungsaufgaben 2023 freigegeben sind, können sie als PDF auf der Plattform MyStark heruntergeladen werden (vgl. Code vorne im Buch).

Autorin: Katharina Menzel

Vorwort

Liebe Schülerin, lieber Schüler,

dieses Buch ist der Lösungsband zu dem Buch ***Original-Prüfungsaufgaben Hauptschule Englisch Hessen*** (Best.-Nr. D06350). Es enthält von mir erstellte kommentierte Lösungen zu den Übungsaufgaben und zu den offiziellen, vom hessischen Kultusministerium gestellten Prüfungsaufgaben des Hauptschulabschlusses 2017–2023. Die Lösungen zum Jahrgang 2023 erscheinen dabei in digitaler Form.
Versuche stets, jede Aufgabe zunächst selbstständig zu lösen, und sieh nicht gleich in der Lösung nach. Solltest du aber nicht weiterkommen, kann ein Blick in die **Lösungen** hilfreich sein. Die Hinweise mit den grauen Rauten informieren dich u. a. darüber, auf was du bei der Bearbeitung einer Aufgabe achten musst und wie die Aufgabe bewertet wird.
Am Schluss solltest du deine Lösung in jedem Fall mit der Lösung in diesem Buch vergleichen. Hast du eine Aufgabe nicht richtig gelöst, lohnt es sich, sie sich zu einem späteren Zeitpunkt nochmals vorzunehmen.
Arbeitest du alle Aufgaben auf diese Weise Schritt für Schritt durch, kann dir in der Prüfung keiner mehr etwas vormachen!

Viel Erfolg wünscht dir

Katharina Menzel

2024

Hauptschulabschluss

Original-Prüfungsaufgaben und Training

Hessen

Englisch

LÖSUNGEN

STARK

20. ergänzte Auflage
www.stark-verlag.de

Hessen Hauptschule – Englisch
Übungsaufgabe 1 – Lösungen

A Listening Comprehension

1. At the airport
Tick (✓) the right statement. There is only one possible answer.

Hinweis: *Vielleicht bist du schon einmal geflogen. Dann werden dir einige Begriffe, die in den Hörtexten und in den Aufgaben enthalten sind, bekannt vorkommen, z. B. „depart/departure" (abfliegen/Abflug) oder „gate" (Flugsteig). Oft wird man auch gefragt, ob man am Fenster („window") oder am Gang („aisle") sitzen möchte.*

a) The call for the flight to Mumbai is the …
- ☐ first call.
- ☐ second call.
- ☑ last call.

b) Diane Miller is …
- ☐ a citizen of New York.
- ☑ coming from New York.
- ☐ leaving for New York.

c) Flight LH 845 leaves from gate …
- ☐ 13.
- ☐ 30.
- ☑ 3.

d) The passenger has got …
- ☐ no hand luggage.
- ☑ a small bag as hand luggage.
- ☐ some bags as hand luggage.

e) The passenger wants to know the number of …
- ☐ the flight.
- ☑ the gate.
- ☐ the counter.

f) The passenger wants to sit …
- ☐ in the middle row.
- ☑ by the window.
- ☐ near the aisle.

g) The check-in clerk has checked the passenger's …
- ☐ boarding ticket.
- ☑ boarding card.
- ☐ board card.

h) The flight attendant announces that the plane will be landing in Mumbai …
- ☐ in four minutes.
- ☐ in few minutes.
- ☑ in a few minutes.

2. Five conversations
Fill in the missing information.

Hinweis: *Hier musst du Sätze mit Wörtern aus den Hörtexten vervollständigen. Versuche, besonders genau zuzuhören, wenn Wörter bzw. Namen buchstabiert werden. Lerne vor der Prüfung daher noch einmal, wie die Buchstaben im englischen Alphabet ausgesprochen werden.*

Conversation 1: Bollywood film
The film Amy is watching is called "**Yaariyan**".

Conversation 2: At the doctor's
The boy tells the doctor that he feels **sick/ill**.

Conversation 3: In the shop
The customer is not sure about the **colour/color** of the dress.

Conversation 4: Hotel reservation
Mr Smith books a room for the **weekend** before Christmas.

Conversation 5: Brother and sister
Daniel doesn't open the door of the bathroom because he has the **music** on too loud.

3. Going on holiday

a) **Part one: Who says what? Write the correct name (John or Sarah) in the chart. Be careful – there is one more statement than you need.**

Hinweis: *Hier musst du John oder Sarah Aussagen zuordnen, die sich auf den ersten Teil des Hörtextes beziehen. Die jeweiligen Aussagen sind manchmal etwas umformuliert, entsprechen aber inhaltlich dem, was John oder Sarah sagen. Eine Aussage lässt sich nicht zuordnen.*

	Statement	Name
A	Australia is too far away and too expensive.	**Sarah**
B	I have never been on another continent.	**John**
C	It would be great to visit a place with a totally different culture.	**John**
D	I don't like Hollywood films.	–
E	Grandma went to Goa in the late 1960s.	**Sarah**

b) **Part two: Tick (✓) the right statement. There is only one possible answer.**

Hinweis: *Die folgenden Aufgaben beziehen sich auf den zweiten Teil des Hörtextes.*

(1) John and Sarah want to go on holiday …

- ☑ for two weeks in autumn.
- ☐ for twelve weeks in autumn.
- ☐ for two weeks in August.

(2) The most interesting things about Goa are …

- ☐ its beaches.
- ☑ its beaches and culture.
- ☐ its culture and nightlife.

(3) The Portuguese left Goa …

- ☐ in the 16th century.
- ☐ in 1916.
- ☑ in 1961.

(4) The agent recommends a hotel. It's …

☐ on the beach.
☑ next to the beach.
☐ far away from the beach.

(5) The hotel has …

☐ free WiFi.
☑ no WiFi.
☐ big flatscreens in the rooms.

(6) John would like to …

☐ do yoga.
☑ visit a big Indian city.
☐ relax in front of the TV.

(7) The trip to India as a package costs …

☐ £ 1,900.
☑ £ 900.
☐ £ 9,000.

B Reading Comprehension

1. Where would you see signs a–c? Tick (✓) the right statement.

Hinweis: *Bei dieser Aufgabe können dir einzelne Wörter schon einen Hinweis auf die richtige Lösung geben, z. B. gibt man Jacken und andere Gegenstände im Museum auf eigene Gefahr („at owner's risk") ab; auch kommt es im Restaurant vor, dass man einen Platz zugewiesen bekommt („wait to be seated"); „For external use only" (nur zur äußeren Anwendung) ergibt hier nur auf der Flasche mit Bodylotion Sinn.*

a)

Jackets and other articles left at owner's risk

☐ at school
☑ in the museum
☐ in a church

b) **Please wait to be seated**

☑ in a restaurant
☐ in a car park
☐ in the cinema

c) **For external use only**

☐ on the dishwasher
☐ on a bar of chocolate
☑ on the bottle of your body lotion

2. An advertisement. Tick (✓) the right statement.

Hinweis: *Folgende Begriffe aus der Stellenanzeige kann man so umschreiben: „speak two languages fluently" = very well; „good communicative skills" bedeutet, dass man offen ist und gut mit Menschen umgehen kann.*

a) The company is looking for a guide …

☐ who wants to stay in the same place.
☑ who loves travelling around.
☐ who is easy-going.

b) When you work as a guide you …

☐ needn't speak foreign languages.
☐ must speak two languages quite well.
☑ must speak two languages very well.

c) You needn't send an application if you …

☐ are friendly.
☐ are hard-working.
☑ don't want to be with other people.

3. India

a) **Match the seven correct headings to each part of the text (1–7).**
Be careful – there is one heading more than you need.

Hinweis: *Bei dieser Aufgabe kommt es auf dein Globalverständnis an, d. h., ob du verstehst, um welches Thema es im jeweiligen Abschnitt geht.*

part of the text	1	2	3	4	5	6	7
heading	**G**	**D**	**E**	**F**	**A**	**C**	**B**

b) **Answer the questions below. Give short answers.**

Hinweis: *Hier musst du den Text noch genauer lesen, denn es wird nach Einzelheiten gefragt. Du musst nicht in ganzen Sätzen antworten; achte jedoch auf Rechtschreibung und Grammatik, sodass deine Antworten verständlich sind.*

How many people live in India's capital city?
more than twenty/20 million people

When did India become independent?
in 1947

What are India's two main official languages?
English and Hindi

What are more than 80 % of the Indian population?
Hindus

What do a lot of Westerners practice in India?
yoga

Which parts of the economy have been growing fast? (Name three items)
the textile industry, the car industry and the IT sector

Whose lives are often very hard in India? (Name three groups of people)
children, women, poor people/members of the lower castes

C Use of Language

1. Mediation

a) **Say it in German.**
Dein Freund/Deine Freundin hat einen Artikel in einer Zeitschrift über ihren/seinen Lieblingsstar gefunden. Da sein/ihr Englisch nicht so gut ist, bittet er/sie dich um Hilfe beim Lesen. Beantworte seine/ihre Fragen auf Deutsch.

Hinweis: *Bei einer Mediationsaufgabe kommt es nicht darauf an, einzelne Stellen wortwörtlich zu übersetzen. Vielmehr sollst du die Information, nach der gefragt ist, in deinen eigenen Worten wiedergeben.*

Super. Wie alt war Gemma denn, als sie das erste Mal in „Happy Hannah“ mitspielte?
12 Jahre

Welche Rolle hat sie nochmal in den „Happy Hannah“-Filmen gespielt?
Hannah Golding

Hier steht, glaube ich, dass Gemma und Hannah viel gemeinsam haben. Was haben sie denn gemeinsam?
Beide sind lebhaft und gut in der Schule.

Gemma war sich nicht sicher, ob sie im letzten Teil mitspielen sollte. Warum?
Sie wusste nicht, ob sie Schule und Film vereinbaren konnte.

Auf welchen Schulabschluss hat sich Gemma vorbereitet?
(Sie hat sich) auf ihren Highschool-Abschluss (vorbereitet.)

Hat ihr die Filmgesellschaft irgendwie geholfen?
Ja, die Filmgesellschaft hat ihr Nachhilfelehrer zur Verfügung gestellt.

Gemma ist ja ziemlich normal geblieben. Wie zeigt sich das?
Sie fällt nicht durch Skandale auf. / Sie ist v. a. mit ihren engen Freunden zusammen.

b) **Say it in English.**
Du bist mit deinen Eltern für ein verlängertes Wochenende in London. Ergänze die folgenden Dialoge mit geeigneten Sätzen oder Fragen. Verwende dabei höfliche Formulierungen.

Hinweis: *Bei dieser Aufgabe werden dir auf Deutsch zwei Situationen beschrieben. Den folgenden Dialog musst du dann auf Englisch vervollständigen. Aus der Beschreibung und den vorgegebenen Antworten kannst du erschließen, was du einfügen musst. Achte auch immer darauf, Höflichkeitsformen zu verwenden, z. B. "I would like to ...", "Could I ...?" etc.*

Situation 1:	**Ihr seid im Hotel und macht euch für den Abend fertig. Du möchtest deine Haare waschen, doch leider habt ihr den Haartrockner zu Hause vergessen. Du fragst an der Rezeption, ob sie dir dort einen geben können.**
Receptionist:	Hello. How can I help you?
You:	**Hello. (I've forgotten my hairdryer at home.) Could I borrow/get a hairdryer?**
Receptionist:	Of course. There must be one in your room.
You:	**(That's great.) Where in the room is it?**
Receptionist:	It's in the drawer of the desk. I'm sorry, it's not so easy to find.

Situation 2:	**Am Abend seid ihr zum Essen in einem Restaurant. Du möchtest gerne eine Cola und fragst, ob es auch einen vegetarischen Burger gibt.**
Waiter:	Hello, what would you like to eat and drink?
You:	**I would like to have a coke and a vegetarian burger/ a burger without meat.**
Waiter:	Yes, of course. There is one with tofu.
You:	**Great, I'll take it.**
Waiter:	OK. One tofu burger for you.
You:	**Can/Could I have it with chips?**
Waiter:	Yes, you can have it with chips.
You:	Great!

2. Words and structures

Hinweis: In der folgenden Aufgabe werden deine Grammatik und dein Wortschatz geprüft.

The best time of your life
Childhood seems to be the best time of our lives. **However**, being a child has both advantages and disadvantages. One advantage is that you have very **few** responsibilities. For example, you **don't** have to go **to** work, pay bills, or **do** the shopping. This means you have a lot of free time. However, you have to go to school **from** Monday to Friday. You also have to **do** homework, and to **pass** exams. In addition, you are not allowed to do **whatever** you want because you **have** to ask your parents.

D Text Production

Hinweis: In der Prüfung kannst du dir eine der Aufgaben zur Textproduktion aussuchen. Es bietet sich jedoch an, zur Vorbereitung auf die Prüfung beide Aufgaben zu bearbeiten.

You have been to the Taj Mahal and you write about your visit in an e-mail to your friend in England.

Hinweis: Sieh dir das Bild mit dem Taj Mahal genau und versuche das, was du darauf siehst, für deine E-Mail zu verwenden. Die folgende Lösung ist ein Beispiel.

Hi Tina,

Greetings from India! I'm having a good time here. Yesterday, I went to see the Taj Mahal. It is hard to describe how I felt when I saw it for the first time: it is so beautiful and huge! We also walked around in the garden. There is a big pool in which the Taj Mahal is reflected. I took a lot of nice photos! You should see the Taj Mahal, too, because it so beautiful.

Love,
Susie

You have won two tickets to an adventure park. But you can't go because you have school. You would like the money for the tickets instead.

Hinweis: Hier musst du eine förmliche E-Mail schreiben. Vergiss daher auf keinen Fall die Anrede und den Schluss. Achte auch darauf, so höflich wie möglich zu schreiben und die entsprechenden Ausdrücke zu verwenden (z. B. "Thank you for…", "I'd like to ask …"). Die folgende Lösung ist ein Beispiel.

Dear Sir or Madam,

Thank you for the tickets to the adventure park. I got them yesterday, and I'm really happy that I won the prize. Unfortunately, I can't go to the adventure park because I have school and my teachers won't give me the day off. So I'd like to ask you if it is possible to have the money instead of the tickets so that I can use it to go to the park in the holidays.

That would be great.

Yours faithfully,
Thomas Schmidt

Hessen Hauptschule – Englisch
Übungsaufgabe 2 – Lösungen

A Listening Comprehension

1. Five announcements
Tick (✓) the right statement. There is only one possible answer.

Hinweis: *Achte bei dieser Aufgabe v. a. auf die Zahlen, die in den Ansagen genannt werden.*

Announcement 1: On a guided bus tour
The skyscraper is …
- ☐ 1776 m high.
- ☐ 2001 m high.
- ☑ 541 m high.

Announcement 2: At a tourist office
The Empire State Building is open …
- ☐ every day from 2 p.m. to 8 p.m.
- ☑ every day from 8 a.m. to 2 a.m.
- ☐ during the week from 8 a.m. to 2 a.m.

Announcement 3: In a railway station
Baggage trolleys are available …
- ☐ for free.
- ☑ for a fee of $ 1.
- ☐ for a fee of £ 1.

Announcement 4: In an underground station
The escalators are out of order …
- ☐ until tomorrow at 8 p.m.
- ☐ until tomorrow at 8 a.m.
- ☑ until today at 8 p.m.

Announcement 5: In a supermarket

For three cans of coke you have to pay …

- [ ] half the price.
- [x] for two only.
- [ ] for two only if you put them into the right bin.

2. Five conversations

Tick (✓) the right statement. There is only one possible answer.

Hinweis: *Lies dir auch hier die Aufgaben genau durch, damit du weißt, auf welche Stichwörter du achten musst. Höre auch wieder genau hin, wenn Wörter bzw. Namen buchstabiert werden.*

Conversation 1: Lost property office

Who was at the lost property office?

- [ ] Mrs Vasnor.
- [x] Mr Vasnor.
- [ ] Mr Wasnor.

Conversation 2: Cinema

The film "Meeting Mr Right" is about …

- [x] love and heartache.
- [ ] crazy squirrels.
- [ ] a gang.

Conversation 3: Glasses

Martha saw the glasses in …

- [ ] the bathroom.
- [x] her husband's shirt pocket.
- [ ] the living room.

Conversation 4: Weekend trip

Susan wants to go to …

- [x] Brighton.
- [ ] London.
- [ ] Stonehenge.

Conversation 5: Coffee shop

The women have …

☐ two hot chocolates with vanilla flavour.

☐ two iced teas.

☑ a latte with vanilla flavour and an iced tea.

3. A trip to the USA

a) **Part one: Tick (✓) the right statement.**

Hinweis: *Diese Aufgaben beziehen sich auf den ersten Teil („Part one") des Hörtextes.*

(1) Jenny is …

☐ on her way to the USA.

☑ flying back home from the United States.

☐ at the airport.

(2) Jenny's surname is …

☐ Jason.

☑ Johnson.

☐ Jackson.

(3) Jenny is talking to …

☐ her neighbour.

☐ the pilot.

☑ a flight attendant.

(4) The flight attendant forgot to bring her …

☑ a vegetarian meal.

☐ pasta bolognese.

☐ curry chicken.

(5) For dessert she takes …

☐ fruit salad.

☐ chocolate cake.

☑ chocolate mousse.

(6) Jenny complains about her …

- [ ] seat.
- [ ] headphones.
- [x] entertainment system.

(7) Jenny …

- [ ] is afraid of flying.
- [x] doesn't want to be bored during the flight.
- [ ] thinks that time will pass quickly.

b) **Part two: Write down six places Jenny visited in the USA and two things she did there. Choose the words from the box. Be careful, there are more words than you need.**

Hinweis: *Die folgende Aufgabe bezieht sich auf den zweiten Teil („Part two") des Hörtextes. Höre genau hin, welche der im Kasten aufgeführten Orte und Aktivitäten genannt werden und schreibe diese in die jeweilige Spalte der Tabelle. Beachte, dass ein paar der angegebenen Begriffe nicht im Hörtext vorkommen.*

places	activities
(1) Niagara Falls	(1) go on top of a skyscraper
(2) Empire State Building	(2) go shopping
(3) Central Park	
(4) Statue of Liberty	
(5) Ellis Island	
(6) Washington D.C.	

B Reading Comprehension

1. Romeo and Juliet

a) **Answer the questions below. Give short answers.**

Hinweis: *Lies dir den Text besonders genau durch, denn hier wird nach Details gefragt. Auch wenn du nicht in ganzen Sätzen antworten musst, solltest du auf Rechtschreibung und Grammatik achten, sodass deine Antworten verständlich sind und somit gewertet werden können.*

Who wrote the story of Romeo and Juliet?
William Shakespeare

Where do Romeo and Juliet meet?
at a party (in Verona)

Who is Tybalt?
Juliet's cousin

Who does Juliet's father want her to marry?
Paris

What does the holy man give to Juliet?
(some) special medicine

Where does Romeo say goodbye to his love?
at Juliet's family tomb (in Verona)

What does Juliet see when she wakes up?
Romeo's dead body

b) **Complete the sentences with words from the text.**

Hinweis: *Gehe den Text noch einmal durch und suche die Stellen, die die Wörter enthalten, mit denen du die angegebenen Sätze sinnvoll vervollständigen kannst.*

Romeo and Juliet's families aren't friends, they are **(bitter) enemies**.
So Romeo and Juliet have to **marry** secretly.
Mercutio, who is **Romeo's friend**, is killed by Tybalt.
After Juliet has taken the medicine she falls **into a deep sleep**.
The holy man arrives **too late** to tell Romeo that Juliet is not dead.
Such is the tragic story about two **teenage lovers**.

2. Social media

a) **The following words have various meanings. Which of the meanings is the one used in the text?**

Hinweis: *Hier werden englische Wörter aus dem Text angegeben, die im Deutschen verschiedene Bedeutungen haben. Du musst nun entscheiden, welche deutsche Übersetzung im Textzusammenhang einen Sinn ergibt. Im zweiten Teil der Aufgabe musst du dann selbst das richtige deutsche Wort einfügen.*

Tick (✓) the correct German meaning. There is only one possible answer.

post (line 4): ☑ online veröffentlichen   *miss* (line 27): ☑ verpassen

Write down the German meaning as used in the text.

imagine (line 1) **(sich etw.) vorstellen**
in person (line 10) **persönlich**
keep (line 24) **bleiben**

b) **Who says what? Fill in the correct names.**

Hinweis: *Lies dir den Text noch einmal gut durch und ordne die Personen den Aussagen zu.*

WHO	thinks social media are important to find a good job?	**Sophie**
	met some really nice people in Spain?	**Oliver**
	always knows what famous people are doing?	**Tina**
	couldn't do without social networks?	**Riley**
	isn't on Facebook any more?	**Jordan**
	isn't really a fan of social networks?	**Daniel**
	thinks that friendship is more than just connecting with people in social networks?	**Amelia**

C Use of Language

1. Mediation

a) **Say it in German.**
Du möchtest mit einem Freund/einer Freundin ein indisches Gericht kochen. Das Rezept ist auf Englisch und dein Freund/deine Freundin möchte wissen, wie ihr das Gericht zubereiten müsst.

Hinweis: *Bei einer Mediationsaufgabe kommt es nicht darauf an, dass du wortwörtlich aus dem Englischen übersetzt, sondern die Informationen, nach denen gefragt wird, in deinen eigenen Worten wiedergibst. Diese Sprachmittlung kannst du auch dazu nutzen, deinen Wortschatz um Begriffe rund um das Kochen zu erweitern.*

Welche Zutaten brauchen wir noch?
Butter/Zwiebeln/Knoblauchzehen/Ingwer/Currypulver/Salz/roten Pfeffer/Cashewkerne/Tomaten/Vollmilchjoghurt/saure Sahne

Hier steht was von Zwiebeln und Knoblauch. Was machen wir damit?
Die Zwiebeln und der Knoblauch müssen ca. 5 Minuten angebraten werden.

Was darf man beim Braten denn auf gar keinen Fall vergessen?
Das Umrühren (darf man nicht vergessen.)

Achja, was kommt denn mit dem Hühnchen noch in den Topf?
(Es kommen noch) Tomaten und Tomatensaft (hinzu.)

Wie lange muss das Hühnchen gekocht werden?
ca. 45 Minuten

Was kann man anstatt Joghurt in die Sauce geben?
(Man kann auch) saure Sahne (nehmen.)

b) **Say it in English.**
Du verbringst deine Sommerferien in Portsmouth, um an einer Sprachenschule dein Englisch zu verbessern. Nach der Schule unternimmst du oft etwas mit den anderen Sprachschülern. Ergänze die folgenden Dialoge mit geeigneten Sätzen oder Fragen.

Hinweis: *Hier sind auf Deutsch zwei Situationen beschrieben. Den folgenden Dialog musst du dann auf Englisch vervollständigen. Aus der Beschreibung und den vorgegebenen Antworten kannst du erschließen, was du einfügen musst. Achte auch immer darauf, Höflichkeitsformen zu verwenden, z. B. "I would like to …", "please" etc.*

Situation 1:	**Ihr wollt am Abend ins Kino gehen. Du rufst dort an, um Karten für einen Film zu reservieren.**
Cinema:	Hello. How can I help you?
You:	**I would like to reserve three tickets for "Return of the Aliens II" at 8 p.m. tonight, please.**
Cinema:	I'm sorry, there are no tickets left for "Return of the Aliens II" at 8 p.m. But I could reserve three tickets for tomorrow night. Would that be OK?
You:	**Yes, that would be OK.**
Cinema:	Great. Then three tickets for tomorrow at 8 p.m.

Situation 2:	**Am Wochenende wollt ihr einen Ausflug nach London unternehmen. Du erkundigst dich am Auskunftsschalter im Bahnhof nach den Zugverbindungen.**
Assistant:	Hello, how can I help you?
You:	**I'd like to know if there are trains to London on Saturday morning.**
Assistant:	Yes, there are. There is at least one train per hour on Saturday morning.
You:	**Where/At which station in London do we arrive?**
Assistant:	You arrive in London at Waterloo Station. Would you like to buy your tickets now?
You:	**No, I've got to ask/talk to my friends first.**
Assistant:	OK, ask your friends first. You can come back here, or book online.

2. Words and structures

Hinweis: *Hier werden deine Grammatik- und Wortschatzkenntnisse geprüft.*

Did you **know** that until 1950 the longest track distance that women **were** permitted to race over was 200 metres? **However**, women have **shown** that they are able **to** run marathons, sail around the world and swim the Channel. They also practise typically male sports nowadays. Girls' football, **for** example, is the **fastest**-growing sport in Britain. Some of the **most** famous schools in the country are playing football **under** professional instruction. In Great Britain, **out** of 500 girls, about 100 play football.

D Text Production

Hinweis: Auch wenn du in der Prüfung nur eine Aufgabe zur Textproduktion auswählst, ist es sinnvoll, zur Vorbereitung auf die Prüfung beide Aufgaben zu bearbeiten.

Tell the story behind the picture.

Hinweis: Sieh dir das Bild genau an und gehe in deinem Text auf alle Punkte ein, die angegeben sind („Wer ist zu sehen?", „Wo befinden sie sich?", „Was passiert?", „Was könnte als Nächstes geschehen?"). Verwende in deinem Text auch Konjunktionen (Bindewörter) wie „and" und „but", um deinen Text „flüssiger" zu gestalten. Der folgende Text ist eine Beispiellösung.

In the picture on the right there is a young woman with short blonde hair and glasses. On the left there is a camel "kissing" the woman. The photo might have been taken in a zoo. The woman is completely taken by surprise because she wasn't expecting a camel to kiss her! You can see that this scene is being filmed by someone holding a smartphone, perhaps a friend of the woman. After having kissed the woman, the camel tries to kiss the woman's friend too, but the friend runs away.

Asking for advice

Hinweis: Vielleicht warst du selbst schon einmal in einer solchen Situation und kannst dich gut in die Person einfühlen, die diese E-Mail schreibt. Der folgende Text ist eine Beispiellösung.

Dear Dr. Summer,

Last Saturday, I met a very nice boy at a friend's party. He also looks so good, and he's so cute. We talked a lot, and he wants to help me with my homework. I'd like to contact him. Do you think that I should phone him or send him an e-mail? Would my house be a good place for our first meeting?
Please help me!

Thank you and best wishes,
Anna

Hessen Hauptschule – Englisch
Übungsaufgabe 3 – Lösungen

A Listening Comprehension

1. Five messages

Tick (✓) the right statement. There is only one possible answer.

Hinweis: *Höre bei den Hörtexten wieder besonders genau hin, wenn Zahlen genannt werden. Wendungen, die du vielleicht noch nicht kennst, sind „due to" (= wegen) und „local time" (= Ortszeit).*

Message 1: At the station

Passengers to London can take bus …

- ☐ no. 2.
- ☐ no. 12.
- ☑ no. 20.

Message 2: Answering machine

Sue Jones can't answer the call because she is …

- ☐ on holiday.
- ☐ at work.
- ☑ not at home.

Message 3: In a plane

The plane lands at Heathrow …

- ☐ at 11.30 Central European time.
- ☑ at 11.30 local time.
- ☐ at 12.30 local time.

Message 4: On the radio

What is this morning's traffic news about?

- ☐ a traffic jam on the M 6.
- ☑ a traffic jam on the M 5.
- ☐ speed checks and a traffic jam on the M 5.

Message 5: In a department store
The restaurant is …

- [ ] on the ground floor next to the sports department.
- [x] on the top floor next to the sports department.
- [ ] in the sports department.

2. Five conversations

Tick (✓) the right statement. There is only one possible answer.

Hinweis: *Höre in „Conversation 3" genau hin, wenn der Name der neuen App buchstabiert wird.*

Conversation 1: At the box office
For students seats cost …

- [ ] £ 20 in the stalls.
- [ ] £ 23 in the gallery.
- [x] £ 15 in the stalls and in the gallery.

Conversation 2: Buying a birthday present
Leo and Sarah are going to treat Sue …

- [ ] to a sports event.
- [x] to the cinema.
- [ ] to a concert.

Conversation 3: New app
The new app's name is …

- [x] Footie2gether.
- [ ] Footie2together.
- [ ] Footi2gether.

Conversation 4: At school
On Mondays Noah's French class …

- [ ] always gets a lot of homework.
- [x] always eats some French food.
- [ ] doesn't have to speak French all the time.

Conversation 5: In the street

To get to the Natural History Museum you have to …

- ☐ walk less than 7 kilometres.
- ☑ turn left into Old Church Street.
- ☐ turn left into Fulham Road.

3. Radio show

a) **Tick (✓) the right statement. There is only one possible answer.**

Hinweis: *Die folgenden Aufgaben beziehen sich auf den ersten und zweiten Teil des Hörtextes.*

(1) The radio show is about …

- ☐ unemployed people.
- ☑ young people and jobs.
- ☐ careers in business.

(2) In the radio show …

- ☑ young people talk about their jobs.
- ☐ people look for a job.
- ☐ companies offer jobs.

(3) Karen Gibbons is …

- ☐ a window cleaner.
- ☑ a window dresser.
- ☐ a dresser.

(4) Karen's job …

- ☐ has nothing to do with the things she likes to do.
- ☐ is her dream job.
- ☑ is not her dream job.

(5) Karen works from …

- ☐ 8.00 to 5.00.
- ☑ 9.00 to 5.00.
- ☐ 5.00 to 9.00.

(6) At weekends she …

- ☐ usually has to work.
- ☑ sometimes has to work.
- ☐ never has to work.

(7) They don't do displays …

- ☐ at weekends.
- ☐ at Christmas.
- ☑ on Mondays.

(8) Karen's salary …

- ☐ is not bad.
- ☑ isn't so good.
- ☐ is about $ 2000 per month.

(9) Karen's plan is …

- ☐ to become an artist.
- ☐ to become a store manager.
- ☑ to be a display manager one day.

b) **Fill in the missing information.**

Hinweis: *Die folgende Aufgabe bezieht sich auf den zweiten Teil des Hörtextes. Bei dieser Einsetzaufgabe musst du während des Hörens genau darauf achten, was („activity") Karen wann bzw. wie oft macht und dann die Zeitangaben („time") vervollständigen.*

activity	**time**
training:	**3/three** years
work from 9.00 to 5.00:	during the **week**
start doing displays:	on **Tuesdays**
clean the shop:	on **Mondays**
be on holiday:	**4/four** weeks a year
take time off:	after a busy **weekend**

B Reading Comprehension

1. Book review

a) **Fill in the grid with <u>one</u> detail per box.**

Hinweis: *Hier fügst du immer nur ein Detail aus dem Text ein. Du musst auch nicht in ganzen Sätzen schreiben und kannst deine Antworten dem Text entnehmen.*

	Malala
place of birth	**(northwest of) Pakistan**
year of birth	1997
at age 11	**began writing a blog**
16th birthday	**speech in front of the United Nations**
at age 17	**(received the) Nobel Peace Prize**
2012	**shot in the head by a Taliban**

b) **Answer the questions below. Give short answers.**

Hinweis: *Lies dir den Text über Malala noch einmal genau durch. Du musst auch hier nicht in ganzen Sätzen antworten; dabei solltest du jedoch auf Rechtschreibung und Grammatik achten, sodass deine Antworten verständlich sind und somit gewertet werden können.*

What is the name of Malala's book?
"I am Malala"

What does Malala fight for?
children's right to education/children's rights

Who believes that girls should have the same right to education as boys?
Malala's father

What did Malala use the name "Gul Makai" for?
to write a blog

What did Malala write about?
about life under the (terror regime of) the Taliban

What did Malala's activism attract?
the hatred of the Taliban

Where does Malala live now?
in England

2. Christmas around the world

a) **The following words have more than one meaning. Which of the meanings is the one used in the text? Tick (✓) the correct German meaning. There is only one possible answer.**

Hinweis: *Hier werden englische Wörter aus dem Text angegeben, die im Deutschen verschiedene Bedeutungen haben. Du musst nun entscheiden, welche deutsche Übersetzung im Textzusammenhang einen Sinn ergibt. Im zweiten Teil der Aufgabe musst du dann selbst das richtige deutsche Wort einfügen.*

spirits (line 21): ☑ Geister   *dish* (line 24): ☑ Gericht

Write down the German meaning as used in the text.

memory (line 8)	Gedenken/Erinnerung
stockings (line 13)	Strümpfe
to believe (line 14)	glauben (an etw.)
sleigh (line 15)	Schlitten

b) **Match the statements and the countries. Fill in the correct country. Write down only one country per box. There is one country more than you need.**

Hinweis: *Lies dir den Text noch einmal gut durch und ordne die Länder den einzelnen Aussagen zu. Ein Land kann keiner Aussage zugeordnet werden.*

Many families have fried chicken as their traditional Christmas dish.	**Japan**
Brooms are hidden at Christmas.	**Norway**
Stockings are hung up over the fireplace.	**UK**
Christmas presents are given at the beginning of the new year.	**Spain**
People decorate their Christmas trees with artificial spider webs.	**Ukraine**
Many people rollerblade to church.	**Venezuela**
The head of the family throws up a spoon of the traditional Christmas dish.	**Slovakia**

C Use of Language

1. Mediation

a) **Say it in German.**
Du hast einen Freund/eine Freundin, der/die einen Artikel in einer Zeitung gelesen hat, ihn aber leider nicht ganz verstanden hat. Beantworte seine/ihre Fragen auf Deutsch.

Hinweis: *Hier kommt es nicht darauf an, wortwörtlich aus dem Englischen zu übersetzen, sondern die Informationen, nach denen gefragt wird, in eigenen Worten wiederzugeben.*

Ich habe nicht verstanden, was etwa 25 % aller Jungs tun würden.
Sie würden sich einer Schönheitsoperation unterziehen.

Aber wieso denn?
Sie möchten so aussehen wie ihre Idole.

Was versprechen sich die Jungs denn von einem guten Aussehen?
Gutes Aussehen würde ihr Leben verbessern, sie hätten mehr Selbstbewusstsein und könnten die Mädchen beeindrucken.

Ich habe verstanden, dass viele Jungs kein Selbstvertrauen haben. Warum?
Bilder von Stars und Kommentare anderer Jungs verunsichern viele. Außerdem können auch Mädchen Druck ausüben.

Hier steht etwas von Kosmetikprodukten. Was haben diese denn mit Jungs zu tun?
Auch Jungs verwenden zunehmend Kosmetikprodukte, z. B. Feuchtigkeitscreme, Selbstbräuner und Haartönung.

b) **Say it in English.**
Du bist mit deiner Familie in den Ferien in Irland. Vervollständige die Dialoge mit passenden Sätzen oder Fragen. Achte darauf, dich höflich auszudrücken.

Hinweis: *Hier sind auf Deutsch zwei Situationen beschrieben. Den folgenden Dialog musst du dann auf Englisch vervollständigen. Aus der Beschreibung und den vorgegebenen Antworten kannst du erschließen, was du einfügen musst. Achte auch immer darauf, Höflichkeitsformen zu verwenden, z. B. "I would like to …" etc.*

Situation 1: **Du bist in einem Kaufhaus und möchtest original irische Souvenirs für deine Freunde zu Hause kaufen. Du fragst am Informationsschalter, wo du diese finden kannst.**

Assistant:	Hello. What can I do for you?
You:	**I'm looking for original Irish souvenirs. Can I buy some here?**
Assistant:	Yes, you can buy original Irish souvenirs here.
You:	**Where do I find/can I buy them**?
Assistant:	Take the escalator up to the third floor. You'll find the souvenir shop on your left.

Situation 2:	**Ihr möchtet euch für einen Tag Fahrräder ausleihen, um einen Küstenfahrradweg entlangzufahren. Du fragst bei einem Fahrradverleih nach, ob ihr vier Fahrräder ausleihen könnt.**
Assistant:	Hello, can I help you?
You:	**Can I rent four bikes for today?**
Assistant:	Yes, of course, we still have four bikes to rent for a day.
You:	**How much would that be?**
Assistant:	That would be € 60 altogether.
You:	**OK. I'll take them.**
Assistant:	Great. Wait a minute, I'll get the bikes …

2. Words and structures

Hinweis: *Hier werden deine Grammatik- und Wortschatzkenntnisse geprüft.*

With a little help from your friends
Do you cheer **up** your friend when he or she is down? Do you notice when he or she **looks** sad? **Does** your friend feel better **after** you have talked to him or her? Then you really are a good friend. What can you do to make your friend **feel** better? You can suggest doing some sport or take your friend **to** the disco. Going **for** a walk often helps, too. When I am sad I **phone** people I haven't **met** for a long time. My grandmother always says, "Don't worry, be happy." And that's what I **do**. Grandmother's advice can help everyone who is sad.

D Text Production

Hinweis: *Auch wenn du in der Prüfung nur eine der Aufgaben zur Textproduktion bearbeiten musst, ist es sinnvoll, zur Vorbereitung auf die Prüfung beide zu machen.*

Advertisement

Hinweis: *Hier sollst du dich selbst beschreiben und die Person, mit der du gerne Sport machen würdest. Der folgende Text ist eine Beispiellösung.*

My name is …, I'm 16 years old and I'm looking for a boy/girl to do sports with me in our town. My hobbies are skateboarding, tennis, swimming and volleyball. I am a member of the local tennis club and I am training for a competition. It would be nice if you could practise with me. I can give you lessons, if you like. I'm sure we'll have a lot of fun together. I also love music and going out. If you are a sporty and fun-loving person, just contact me.

Text message

Hinweis: *Vielleicht warst du schon einmal in einer ähnlichen Situation und musstest einen Freund/eine Freundin bei Liebeskummer trösten. Überlege, wie du Julia wieder aufmuntern kannst. Der folgende Text ist eine Beispiellösung.*

Hi Julia,

I can't believe it! Why did Marc leave you? But don't be sad, he wasn't the right boy for you anyway. Don't worry, you'll soon find a new boyfriend, who will be much nicer than Marc. What is important is not to phone Marc or send a text to him now!
What do you think about going to Lisa's party tomorrow? That will take your mind off Marc. By the way, I can ask Brad to come with us …

Love,
Anna

Hessen Hauptschule – Englisch
Übungsaufgabe 4 – Lösungen

A Listening Comprehension

1. Five announcements
Tick (✓) the right statement. There is only one possible answer.

Announcement 1: Department store

Today you can taste …

- [ ] cosmetics.
- [ ] chocolate.
- [x] cheese.

Announcement 2: In a museum

The elevator in the modern gallery …

- [ ] is at the north side of the building.
- [x] can't be used at the moment.
- [ ] closes in ten minutes.

Announcement 3: At school

There are still tickets for …

- [x] the school orchestra and choir.
- [ ] the school orchestra.
- [ ] the school choir.

Announcement 4: Shopping mall

In the summer sale you can buy …

- [ ] clothes for 70 % less.
- [ ] sandals and sneakers for half the price.
- [x] sneakers and sandals for up to 70 % less.

Announcement 5: Hotline

CineStar gives information about special events if you press …

- ☐ 1.
- ☐ 2.
- ☑ 3.

2. Five conversations

Tick (✓) the right statement. There is only one possible answer.

Hinweis: *Höre auch hier wieder besonders genau hin, wenn Zahlen genannt werden oder wenn ein Name buchstabiert wird.*

Conversation 1: Telephone number

The telephone number of Peter Waller is …

- ☑ 0473923434.
- ☐ 0473923443.
- ☐ 0473924434.

Conversation 2: Facebook message

Laura didn't see what Jenny posted on Facebook because …

- ☐ she was having a pizza.
- ☐ she was buying a jacket at Cara's.
- ☑ the reception was bad.

Conversation 3: Hairdresser's

The caller's name is …

- ☐ Jamie.
- ☑ Jamilah.
- ☐ Jalimah.

Conversation 4: Doctor's appointment

The caller has an appointment …

- ☐ on Thursday 24th May at 6 p.m.
- ☑ on Tuesday 24th May at 6 p.m.
- ☐ on Tuesday 24th May at 6 a.m.

Conversation 5: Tourist office

The White Swan Hotel …

- [ ] is not far from London's sights.
- [ ] is not far from Edinburgh.
- [x] is not far from Edinburgh's sights.

3. The meteorite

Hinweis: *Die folgende Aufgabe bezieht sich auf den ersten Teil des Hörtextes.*

a) **Part one: Fill in the missing information.**

Name of the show's presenter:	**Tina Smith**
Name of the show:	"**Strange** things happen"
Sam and Lisa's last name:	**McDonald**
Sam and Lisa are from:	Phoenix, **Arizona**
Time of the meteorite crash:	**9 o'clock in the morning / 9 a.m.**
Weight of the meteorite:	**1.3 kg**
Where the meteorite landed:	**(in the) living room**
What happened to the McDonalds is:	very **rare**

b) **Part two: Tick (✓) the right answer.**

Hinweis: *Diese Aufgaben beziehen sich auf den zweiten Teil des Hörtextes.*

(1) When the meteorite came down …

- [ ] Sam was preparing breakfast in the kitchen.
- [x] Lisa was preparing breakfast in the kitchen.
- [ ] Lisa and Sam were in their living room.

(2) There was …

- [ ] a horrible explosion.
- [x] a huge explosion.
- [ ] no explosion.

(3) In the kitchen …

- [x] there was dust everywhere.
- [ ] there were parts of the ceiling everywhere.
- [ ] there was the meteorite.

(4) A rock was lying under …
- ☐ the roof.
- ☐ the sofa.
- ☑ the computer.

(5) The McDonalds put the rock …
- ☐ into the fridge so that it could cool down.
- ☑ into the oven so that it could dry out.
- ☐ in a museum.

(6) The meteorite could be worth …
- ☐ thousand dollars.
- ☐ seven thousand dollars.
- ☑ several thousand dollars.

(7) Lisa and Sam are planning to give the rock to …
- ☐ collectors.
- ☑ a museum.
- ☐ meteorite-hunters.

B Reading Comprehension

1. The World Wide Web

a) **Match the seven correct headings to each part of the text (1–5). Be careful – there is one heading more than you need.**

Hinweis: *Bei dieser Aufgabe kommt es auf dein Globalverständnis an, d. h., ob du verstehst, um welches Thema es im jeweiligen Abschnitt geht.*

part of the text	1	2	3	4	5
heading	**F**	**E**	**D**	**A**	**C**

b) **Answer the questions below. Give short answers.**
Hinweis: *Lies den Text genau durch, denn hier wird nach Details gefragt. Es reicht, wenn du in Stichpunkten antwortest. Du kannst deine Antworten dem Text entnehmen – achte dabei jedoch auf die richtige Schreibung, denn nur korrekte und verständliche Antworten zählen.*

When did the World Wide Web start?
in the early 1990s

Who developed the World Wide Web?
Tim Berners-Lee

Where was the World Wide Web developed?
at CERN (European Organization for Nuclear Research in Geneva)

What was special about the World Wide Web? (Name two things)
free of charge and easy to use

Since what date has the World Wide Web been open to everyone?
April 30, 1993

Who made the developer of the World Wide Web a knight?
Queen Elizabeth II

2. Music

a) **The following words have more than one meaning. Which of the meanings is the one used in the text? Tick (✓) the correct German meaning. There is only one possible answer.**

Hinweis: *Hier werden englische Wörter aus dem Text angegeben, die im Deutschen verschiedene Bedeutungen haben. Du musst nun entscheiden, welche deutsche Übersetzung im Textzusammenhang einen Sinn ergibt. Im zweiten Teil der Aufgabe musst du dann selbst das richtige deutsche Wort einfügen.*

since (line 21) ☑ seit   *effect* (line 27) ☑ Wirkung

Write down the German meaning as used in the text.

mood (line 3)	Laune/Stimmung
stage (line 13)	Bühne
turn on (line 15)	anschalten/anmachen
discover (line 32)	entdecken

b) **Fill in the correct names. Write down only <u>one</u> name per box. There is one more person than you need.**

WHO	was touched by someone's music?	**Amelia**
	isn't really interested in music?	**Thomas**
	is a fan of hip hop and rap music?	**Mason**
	is addicted to music?	**Harry**
	makes music herself?	**Grace**
	is going to a concert?	**Amber**
	likes cheerful music?	**Holly**

C Use of Language

1. Mediation

a) **Say it in German.**
Du möchtest mit einem Freund/einer Freundin einige Zeit im Ausland verbringen. Im Internet hast du eine Organisation gefunden, die Auslandsaufenthalte organisiert. Dein Freund/Deine Freundin kann nicht so gut Englisch und du beantwortest seine/ihre Fragen.

Hinweis: *Achte hier wieder darauf, die Informationen in deinen eigenen Worten wiederzugeben, also so, wie du auch auf die Fragen von einem Freund antworten würdest, z. B. „Man hilft …“, „Auf der Homepage gibt es …“. Du musst nicht immer in ganzen Sätzen antworten.*

Welche Möglichkeiten des Auslandsaufenthaltes gibt es denn?
Praktika, „Work and travel“ (Verbindung von Arbeiten und Reisen), Schüleraustausch und Freiwilligenarbeit

Was genau macht man bei „volunteer work“?
Man hilft Menschen in Entwicklungsländern (z. B. in Schulen oder Krankenhäusern).

Wie lange dauern die einzelnen Programme?
von ein paar Wochen bis zu einem Jahr

Wo finden die Programme statt?
fast überall auf der Welt

Gibt es auch Erfahrungsberichte von früheren Teilnehmern? Wenn ja, wo kann man sie finden?
Ja, die gibt es. Auf der Homepage der Organisation findest du Erfahrungsberichte früherer Teilnehmer.

b) **Say it in English.**
Du bist auf Schüleraustausch und wohnst bei einer englischen Gastfamilie. Vervollständige die Dialoge mit passenden Sätzen oder Fragen. Achte darauf, dich höflich auszudrücken.
Hinweis: *Hier sind auf Deutsch zwei Situationen beschrieben. Den folgenden Dialog musst du dann auf Englisch vervollständigen. Aus der Beschreibung und den vorgegebenen Antworten kannst du erschließen, was du einfügen musst. Achte auch immer darauf, Höflichkeitsformen zu verwenden, z. B. "I would like to …", "Could I …" etc.*

Situation 1:	**Du möchtest alleine mit dem Bus in die Innenstadt fahren. Du findest jedoch nicht die richtige Bushaltestelle. Also fragst du einen Passanten.**
You:	**Excuse me, could you help me?**
Man:	Yes, of course. What do you want to know?
You:	**I would like to go to the city centre (by bus). Could you tell me where the next bus stop is?**
Man:	Oh, that's easy. The bus stop is just around the corner. You have to take the 58.
You:	**Thank you (very much).**
Man:	You're welcome. Have a nice day.

Situation 2:	**Du bist in der Touristeninformation und möchtest fünf Postkarten kaufen. Du sagst, dass die Karten nach Deutschland gehen, und du erkundigst dich, ob du auch Briefmarken dazu kaufen kannst.**
Assistant:	Hello, how can I help you?
You:	**I would like to buy five postcards.**
Assistant:	Five postcards – that's £2.
You:	**The cards are going to Germany. Do you also sell stamps? / Can I also buy stamps here?**
Assistant:	Yes, of course. That'll be £4 with the stamps.
You:	Here you are. **Thank you (very much).**
Assistant:	You're welcome. Bye!

2. Words and structures

Hinweis: *Hier werden dein Wortschatz und deine Grammatikkenntnisse geprüft.*

The lost cat

Blacky the cat **came** back to her owners after two years. They thought they would never see her **again**. She was in the garden when someone **stole** her. An animal rights organization **found** her when they heard about people treating a cat **badly**. The organization scanned the cat **for** a microchip. The cat had one. Thanks to microchipping a lot of cats and dogs **have** been found. Unfortunately, animal organizations have to find new homes for many animals because **there** is no way **of** finding their owners. Hopefully, in the future all pets **will** have microchips.

D Text Production

Hinweis: *In der Prüfung musst du nur eine der beiden Aufgaben zur Textproduktion bearbeiten. Damit du so viel Übung wie möglich bekommst, ist es jedoch sinnvoll, zur Vorbereitung auf die Prüfung beide Aufgaben zu bearbeiten.*

Modern communication

Hinweis: *Der Cartoon veranschaulicht, dass sich durch die Smartphones das Kommunikationsverhalten vieler Menschen geändert hat. Anstatt direkt miteinander zu sprechen, wird oft nur über Apps miteinander kommuniziert. In einem kurzen Text sollst du darauf eingehen, wie du selbst das Smartphone gebrauchst. Gehe dabei auf alle Punkte in der Angabe ein. Der folgende Text ist eine Beispiellösung.*

I use my smartphone every day from morning to evening. I tell my friends when I feel good or bad, but I think that we use our smartphones too often. It would be better to meet people instead of phoning them or sending them messages. Smartphones can also make you lazy. You needn't think about things, for example, because you have an alarm which reminds you of everything. Many people also don't read books anymore because they can look up everything on their little computer.

Trip to London

Hinweis: *Hier musst du einen kurzen Text zu einem Aufenthalt in London schreiben, den du gewonnen hast. Gehe auf alle Punkte ein, die in der Angabe aufgelistet sind. Die folgende Lösung ist eine Beispiellösung.*

A fantastic trip to London

I won a three-day trip to London in your competition. Nobody can imagine how happy I was when I got the letter with the tickets! The trip was great. I went with my mother, and we visited all the famous places in London, such as Buckingham Palace, the Tower and Madame Tussauds. I was also able to practise my English a lot. On my next trip to London I will take my friends with me, too.

Abschlussprüfungen an Hauptschulen in Hessen 2017
Englisch

A Listening Comprehension

1. Announcements

Tick (✓) the right statement. There is only one possible answer per statement.

Hinweis: *Für jede richtige Antwort bekommst du einen Punkt. Kreuze aber nicht einfach mehrere Antworten an – dafür erhältst du keinen Punkt.*

Text 1: At a hotel

Breakfast is either at
- ☐ 7:00, 7:30 or 8:00.
- ☐ 7:45, 8:30 or 8:45.
- ☑ 7:00, 7:45 or 8:30.

To get to the swimming pool, you should walk past the bar,
- ☐ go up the stairs and then turn left.
- ☑ go down the stairs and then turn left.
- ☐ turn left through the double doors and then right.

Text 2: At the reception desk

In the hotel room, there is
- ☑ a minibar, a bathroom and a safe box.
- ☐ a minibar, a bathroom and a laptop.
- ☐ a minibar, a safe box and lemonade.

You cannot connect to the Internet
- ☐ at the pool.
- ☑ in the restaurant.
- ☐ at the reception.

Aqua-jogging is on
- ☐ Tuesday, Thursday and Saturday.
- ☐ Sunday, Tuesday and Friday.
- ☑ Monday, Wednesday and Friday.

Text 3: On the ferry

The Lighthouse Café is on
- ☐ Deck 8 at the front of the boat.
- ☑ Deck 7 at the back of the boat.
- ☐ Deck 7 in the middle of the boat.

The shop offers
- ☐ beers, perfume and music.
- ☐ tobacco, beer and perfume.
- ☑ wines, perfume and chocolate.

Text 4: In a restaurant

Dave orders
- ☐ spaghetti Bolognese.
- ☑ the all-day English breakfast.
- ☐ fish and chips.

Dad drinks
- ☑ coffee.
- ☐ cola.
- ☐ orange juice.

Das has to pay
- ☐ £ 27.80.
- ☐ € 23.20.
- ☑ £ 23.20.

2. Conversation: The weekend
Tick (✓) the right statement. There is only one possible answer per statement.

Hinweis: *Für jede richtige Antwort bekommst du einen Punkt. Wenn du mehrere Antworten ankreuzt, erhältst du keinen Punkt.*

(1) On Friday night, Steve
- ☐ wanted a night in.
- ☐ went out.
- ☑ mended his car.

(2) Finally, he watched a ____ on TV.
- ☐ western film
- ☑ horror movie
- ☐ romantic comedy

(3) Rachel stayed in the Game Bar for
- ☐ one hour.
- ☐ two hours.
- ☑ three hours.

(4) Rachel says 'Ticket to Ride' is
- ☐ easy to play.
- ☑ a thrilling game.
- ☐ unexciting.

(5) Planet Bounce is open on Saturdays until
- ☐ 7 pm.
- ☑ 9 pm.
- ☐ 10 pm.

(6) To jump, you need
- ☑ special socks.
- ☐ a safety helmet.
- ☐ hand protectors.

(7) Rachel's mum bought herself a ______ dress.
- ☐ blue
- ☑ yellow
- ☐ black

(8) For next weekend, Rachel and Steve decide to go to
- ☑ an art show.
- ☐ a Spanish restaurant.
- ☐ the countryside.

3. Radio interview

Fill in the answers with one detail per box.

Hinweis: *Hier bekommst du für jede Antwort, die sinngemäß richtig und lesbar ist, einen Punkt (halbe Punkte werden nicht vergeben). Du musst dabei keine ganzen Sätze schreiben. Rechtschreib- und Grammatikfehler werden nicht gewertet.*

Liza's hobby	**surfing**
why she likes it	**cool/exciting (sport)**
when she does her hobby	**(every) Saturday**
who with	**(her) boyfriend**
age when she started	**12/twelve**
cost of a lesson	**(about) $ 80/80 Dollars (an hour)**
Liza's job	**DJ**

B Reading Comprehension

1. A year in space

a) **Match the six correct headings to each part of the text (1–6).**
Be careful – there is one heading more than you need.

Hinweis: *Für jede richtige Zuordnung bekommst du einen Punkt.*

part of the text	1	2	3	4	5	6
heading	**E**	**C**	**G**	**D**	**A**	**F**

b) **Answer the questions below. Give short answers.**

Hinweis: *Hier erhältst du für jede Antwort, die sinngemäß richtig und lesbar ist, einen Punkt (halbe Punkte werden nicht vergeben). Du musst dabei keine ganzen Sätze schreiben. Rechtschreib- und Grammatikfehler werden nicht gewertet.*

What happened on March 2nd, 2016?
History was made./A Russian spacecraft landed in Kazakhstan.

How many times did Kelly and Kornienko go around Earth during the mission?
5,440 (times)

What did Scott Kelly do to have fun on the space station? (one detail)
(He) did stunts/fooled around/wore a gorilla suit/chased Timothy Peake/played ping-pong (with water drops)/(did 360°) flips.

What did Kelly miss in space? (one detail)
(spending time with) family/swimming/(eating) fresh food

Name one health problem Kelly had on his trip.
(He) grew thin/lost muscle/(had) problems with (his) blood circulation.

Why are scientists testing Kelly's twin brother as well?
to compare differences in health

2. Things to do in your school holidays

a) **The following words have more than one meaning.**
Which of the meanings is the one used in the text?
Tick (✓) the correct German meaning. There is only one possible answer.

Hinweis: Für jede richtige Antwort gibt es einen Punkt. Wenn du mehrere Antworten ankreuzt, erhältst du keinen Punkt.

turn (line 15): ☑ umwandeln
still (line 31): ☑ noch immer

Write down the German meaning as used in the text.

***Hinweis:** Hier ergibt jede sinngemäß richtige Antwort einen Punkt. Rechtschreibfehler werden nicht gewertet. Achte aber darauf, die richtige Wortart zu wählen, sonst gibt es keinen Punkt (z. B.: „change" ist hier ein Nomen und kein Verb).*

change (line 11): **Veränderung/Wechsel**

cases (line 14): **Etui(s)/Hülle(n)**

off (line 18): **frei/weg**

takes (line 20): **brauchen/braucht/erfordern/erfordert**

memory (line 27): **Speicher(kapazität)**

b) **Fill in the correct tip numbers. Write down only <u>one</u> number per box. Be careful – there is one tip more than you need.**

***Hinweis:** Für jede richtige Zuordnung bekommst du einen Punkt.*

Which tip tells you to	invite your friends for films?	**2**
	complete a project?	**4**
	clean and organize?	**6**
	visit a place nearby?	**3**
	try something like a paperback bestseller?	**7**
	be creative in the kitchen?	**1**

C Use of Language

1. Mediation

a) **Say it in German.**

***Hinweis:** Für jede Antwort, die verständlich und sinngemäß richtig ist, bekommst du einen Punkt (halbe Punkte werden nicht vergeben). Du musst keine vollständigen Sätze schreiben. Achte darauf, hier auf Deutsch zu antworten, Antworten auf Englisch zählen nicht.*

Kannst du mit mir mal über Flyer schauen? Leider verstehe ich nicht alles. Was ist denn anders als in einem gewöhnlichen Restaurant?
Man isst im Dunkeln/wird von Blinden bedient./(Es ist eine) Mischung aus (einer) Show und (einem) Essen im Dunkeln.

Aha. Woher wissen wir denn eigentlich, wie genau der Aufenthalt dort abläuft?
Man bekommt alles (15 Minuten) vorher erklärt.

Du weißt ja, dass deine Cousine kein Fleisch isst. Was kann sie denn zum Essen bestellen?
ein vegetarisches („grünes") Menü

OK. Prima. Aber woher weiß denn der Kellner, dass ich etwas bestellen möchte oder eine Frage habe?
(Du musst) die Bedienung beim (Vor)namen rufen.

Wie ungewöhnlich. Du weißt ja, dass mir manchmal etwas mulmig wird, wenn ich mich nicht selbst orientieren kann. Was passiert denn dann?
(Du musst die) Bedienung rufen. / (Die) Bedienung begleitet dich ans Tageslicht.

Gut, das beruhigt mich. Müssen wir vorab einen Tisch reservieren oder können wir einfach spontan unser Glück versuchen?
(Es) muss unbedingt (ein Tisch) reserviert/vorbestellt werden.

OK. Du weißt ja, dass wir abends gerne so früh wie möglich essen gehen. Wann können wir denn dort frühestens essen?
(Ihr könnt ab/um) 18.30 Uhr/halb sieben (dort essen.)

Super. Gibt es Dinge, die wir nicht mit an den Tisch nehmen dürfen? (2 Informationen)
Taschen / Mäntel / Handys / Feuerzeuge / alles, was Licht produziert

Verstehe. Wo in London finden wir das Restaurant?
29–30 Kane Street/nahe/in der Nähe der neuen Farringdon Station

Das liegt ja sogar in der Nähe unseres Hotels. Toll! Ich danke dir für deine Hilfe.
Gern geschehen. Viel Spaß!

b) **Say it in English.**

Hinweis: *Lies dir die Angabe und die Situationen genau durch, denn nur für eine verständliche und sinngemäß richtige Antwort bekommst du einen Punkt. Bei Rechtschreibfehlern bekommst du keine Punkte abgezogen. Eine Lösung, die durch Grammatikfehler nicht mehr verständlich ist, wird jedoch nicht gewertet. Achte auch darauf, höfliche Wendungen zu benutzen, andernfalls wird ein halber Punkt abgezogen.*

Situation 1:

You:	Excuse me, please. (1) **Is this the (correct/right) way to the Roman Baths?**
Man:	Hi. Yes, of course. Go down Westgate Street and then turn right into Union Street. Walk along Union Street. The Roman Baths are on the left.
You:	(2) **Thank you (very much). /Thanks. Are the Baths already open?**
Man:	Let me see. It's quarter to nine now. I think they open at nine o'clock.
You:	OK. Thank you very much for your help.

Situation 2:

Assistant:	Hello, how can I help you?
You:	Good morning, (1) **(I'd like to buy) three tickets, please./ (Could/Can I have/buy) three tickets, please?**
Assistant:	OK. That's £45, please.
You:	(2) **Is there a (price) reduction/discount for teenagers?/ Do teenagers get a (price) reduction/discount?**
Assistant:	Yes, of course. Then it's £44.50. But in that case I recommend a family ticket for £44.
You:	Oh, OK. Here you are. (3) **Do you have/Could/Can I have a brochure?**
Assistant:	Certainly. You can find all important information in seven different languages in it. Enjoy your visit!
You:	Thank you very much.

2. Words and structures

Choose the correct options and fill in the gaps.

Hinweis: *Für jede richtige Antwort gibt es einen Punkt. Bei Rechtschreibfehlern bekommst du jedoch keinen Punkt.*

Juno

Juno is a spacecraft designed and operated **by** NASA, the US space agency. It **was** launched from Cape Canaveral on August 5th, 2011 and is 3.5 metres in height. When **its** wings are open, Juno is more than 20 metres wide.
The spacecraft gets its name from Juno, who in Roman mythology was queen of the gods. She was married **to** the king, Jupiter.
He wasn't **always** well-behaved and Juno often looked down through the clouds to **see** what he was doing. This is also what the spacecraft will do – it will look through the clouds that cover the surface of the planet Jupiter.
Jupiter is the **largest** planet in our solar system. It is two and a half times larger **than** all the other planets in our solar system combined. The planet turns at high speed, completing one turn **every** ten hours.
Thanks to this mission, it will be the **first** time that humans will see what lies beneath Jupiter's cloudy atmosphere. The main aim is to understand how the planet formed and evolved, which in turn **will give** us more information about the rest of the solar system.

http://jumpmag.co.uk/what-is-juno/

D Text Production

***Hinweis**: Hier musst du <u>eine</u> der beiden Aufgaben bearbeiten. Wähle die Aufgabe, zu der dir am meisten einfällt. Gehe auf alle Punkte ein, die angegeben sind. Orientiere dich an der vorgegebenen Wortanzahl. Die folgenden Lösungen sind Beispiele.*

My favourite activity

My favourite activity is playing handball in a club because I can meet all my friends who like sport there. We practice in our school gym every Friday, but sometimes we have extra training before important matches. These matches make me very excited. Our coach is young, nice and good-looking. He always helps us when there are problems. I also like handball because I am a team player, and I can keep my body fit. That's why I have a good mark in PE.

Write a text about the picture

In the picture, there are two older people, a man and a woman. Maybe they are a couple who live in a retirement home, and they went outside in the park. The woman is on a skateboard. In one hand, she is holding an umbrella, and the man is holding her other hand, helping her to stay on the skateboard; but the man is telling her to try skateboarding without help. The woman looks a bit scared, but finally she manages to stand on the skateboard on her own!

Abschlussprüfungen an Hauptschulen in Hessen 2018
Englisch

A Listening Comprehension

1. Message on an answering machine
Fill in the missing information.

Hinweis: Hier musst du jeweils das richtige Wort einfügen, um den Satz zu vervollständigen. Deine Lösung muss verständlich und sinngemäß richtig sein – nur dann bekommst du einen Punkt.

They are going to pick Melissa up on **Monday** at 7.30.
Melissa must bring her **speakers**.
Eve has bought a **(pink) lipstick**.

2. Conversation at the youth hostel
Tick (✓) the right statement. There is only one possible answer per statement.

Hinweis: Für jede richtige Antwort bekommst du einen Punkt. Wenn du mehrere Antworten ankreuzt, bekommst du keinen Punkt.

Text 1: At the reception desk

(1) The class will stay for ____ nights.
- ☐ 3
- ☑ 4
- ☐ 5

(2) They leave out the
- ☐ hiking trip.
- ☐ sightseeing tour.
- ☑ rafting tour.

(3) The pool is open from
- ☑ 10 am to 8 pm.
- ☐ 11 am to 7 pm.
- ☐ 10 am to 11 pm.

(4) Tonight's vegetarian meal is
- ☑ pasta with a mushroom sauce.
- ☐ tofu sausage, chips and beans.
- ☐ veggie burger, chips and peas.

Text 2: Planning the stay

(1) Toby doesn't like
- ☐ minigolf.
- ☑ swimming
- ☐ biking.

(2) Eve has got _____ in her bag.
- ☑ shampoo, shower gel and toothpaste
- ☐ shampoo, toothpaste and a toothbrush
- ☐ shower gel, make-up and a toothbrush

(3) Gordon is sharing a room with
- ☐ Ben and Luke.
- ☐ Ben and Sam.
- ☑ Ben and Toby.

(4) They will go to town
- ☐ this afternoon.
- ☐ tomorrow morning.
- ☑ tomorrow afternoon.

3. Survey

Listen to these people talking about Brexit. Who says what? Write the correct letters in the chart. Be careful – there is one statement more than you need.

Hinweis: *Für jede richtige Zuordnung bekommst du einen Punkt. Beachte, dass eine Aussage nicht zugeordnet werden kann.*

John	Lucy	Maddy	Tom	Olivia	Kate	Stefanie
F	**A**	**E**	**G**	**H**	**B**	**D**

4. Phone call

Fill in the missing information.

Hinweis: *Hier musst du die richtigen Lösungen in ein Formular einfügen. Jede Antwort, die sinngemäß richtig und verständlich ist, ergibt einen Punkt. In der Lösung sind verschiedene Möglichkeiten aufgeführt, das Datum anzugeben. Rechtschreibfehler werden nicht gewertet, jedoch muss der buchstabierte Name richtig notiert werden.*

Smithson Job Agency, Sheffield
– application form –

job:	**hairdresser**
name:	**Imogen** (first name) **Shaw** (last name)
address:	**7 Bishop Street** Sheffield
phone number:	**07493 443890**
date of birth:	**9th September 2001 / 9 September 2001 / 9/9/2001**
can start from:	**25th June / 25 June**

B Reading Comprehension

1. The *Great British Bake Off*

a) **Match the six correct headings to each part of the text (1–6). Be careful – there is one heading more than you need.**

Hinweis: *Für jede richtige Zuordnung bekommst du einen Punkt. Beachte, dass eine Überschrift nicht zugeordnet werden kann.*

part of the text	1	2	3	4	5	6
heading	**C**	**E**	**A**	**B**	**G**	**F**

b) **Answer the questions below. Give short answers.**

Hinweis: *Hier musst du keine vollständigen Sätze schreiben. Achte jedoch darauf, dass deine Antworten verständlich sind, auch wenn Rechtschreib- und Grammatikfehler nicht gewertet werden.*

What is the *Great British Bake Off* (GBBO)?
a (British) television baking competition/a TV baking show

How long do the episodes last?
1/one hour

What was Candice Brown's job before she won the GBBO?
a (PE) teacher

Where did Candice grow up?
in (her parents') pubs/in London

Which great opportunities were offered to her after she had won the show? (Name one.)
- **(writing) her own cook book /**
- **(being the star in) her own TV baking show /**
- **(opening) her own tea shop**

Name one effect of the show's success.
- **(It has) become part of British culture. /**
- **Interest in home baking has grown. /**
- **(The) sales of baking ingredients/baking books/baking accessories (have) increased. /**
- **(There are) now more than 20 different international versions of the show.**

2. Seven tips for Las Vegas

a) **The following words have more than one meaning. Which of the meanings is the one used in the text? Tick (✓) the correct German meaning. There is only one possible answer.**

objects (line 5):	☑	Gegenstände
past (line 6):	☑	vorbei an
steel (line 11):	☑	Stahl

Write down the German meaning as used in the text.

Hinweis: *Überlege, was das jeweilige Wort im Satzzusammenhang bedeutet, um eine sinngemäß richtige Antwort zu geben. Auch muss sie verständlich sein, obwohl Rechtschreib- und Grammatikfehler nicht gewertet werden. Verwendest du in deiner Antwort die falsche Wortart, bekommst du keinen Punkt.*

rows (line 8):	**Reihen**
drive (line 14):	**Fahrt/Fahrzeit**
year-round (line 17):	**ganzjährig / das ganze Jahr hindurch/über**
stretch (line 25):	**Fluss(abschnitt)/Abschnitt/Strecke**

b) **Fill in the correct tip number. Write down only one tip number per box. Be careful – there is one tip more than you need.**

Hinweis: *Achte hier darauf, dass ein Tipp nicht passt.*

Where can you see	a good place for a science-fiction movie?	**3**
	cool stores?	**6**
	a masterpiece of engineering?	**4**
	objects from Las Vegas' past?	**1**
	things from the bottom of the sea?	**7**
	animals in nature?	**5**

C Use of Language

1. Mediation

a) **Say it in German.**

Hinweis: *Bei der folgenden Mediation musst du nicht unbedingt vollständige Sätze schreiben. Achte jedoch darauf, dass deine Antworten verständlich und sinngemäß richtig sind. Für Antworten auf Englisch bekommst du keine Punkte.*

Ich würde gerne einmal dort klettern gehen! Was passiert denn, bevor wir loslegen dürfen?
(Man bekommt vom Personal) eine Sicherheitsunterweisung.

Ich bin noch nie geklettert! Was passiert, wenn ich während des Kletterns Probleme bekomme?
Das Personal (ist im Wald unterwegs und) kann helfen./
Man kann andere auch einfach überholen lassen.

OK. Welcher Pfad ist denn dann für mich als Anfängerin geeignet?
Tree Top Fun

Alles klar. Ich werde bestimmt trotzdem lange brauchen. Was passiert denn, wenn ich zu langsam bin?
Du lässt andere (einfach) an dir vorbei. / Gar nichts.

Was muss ich bei meiner Kleidung beachten? (2 Informationen)
Kleidung anziehen, die schmutzig werden darf / Regenmantel / nichts Bauchfreies / geeignetes Schuhwerk (mit griffigen Sohlen) / keine Sandalen

Was passiert bei Sturm?
Bei Sturm schließen sie/wird geschlossen.

Was muss ich beachten, wenn ich einen Fotoapparat mitnehmen möchte?
(Du musst ihn) an der Kleidung festmachen.

Das ist mir zu riskant. Was soll ich denn dann am besten mit meinen Wertsachen machen?
zu Hause lassen

Gut, dann lass uns das jetzt buchen. Wie geht das denn am einfachsten?
über einen Link auf der Internetseite

Super, ich freue mich schon!

b) **Say it in English.**

Hinweis: *Lies dir die Aufgabenstellung und die Situationen 1 und 2 genau durch, denn nur für eine verständliche und sinngemäß richtige Antwort bekommst du einen Punkt. Bei Rechtschreibfehlern bekommst du keine Punkte abgezogen. Ist die Lösung durch Grammatikfehler nicht mehr verständlich, wird sie jedoch nicht gewertet. Achte auch darauf, dich höflich auszudrücken!*

Situation 1:

Assistant:	Hello. Do you need any help?
You:	Yes, please. (1) **My suitcase hasn't arrived.**
Assistant:	Oh, I'm very sorry. May I check your ticket for your registration number, please? What does your suitcase look like?
You	(2) **It is red and there is/it has a blue sticker on the/its side.**
Assistant:	OK. Thank you. I've entered the details into our system. Here's your reference number. We'll call you as soon as we've found your suitcase. I'm sorry for the inconvenience.
You:	Thank you very much for your help.

Situation 2:

Ms Miller:	Hello. This is Angela Miller from the airport luggage office speaking. We've found your suitcase. It was on the wrong luggage belt.
You:	Hello. Oh, that's great. (1) **Shall I come and pick up/get my suitcase?**
Ms Miller:	Oh, no. We'll send it to your hotel.
You:	OK. (2) **When will it arrive/be at the hotel?**
Ms Miller:	The courier will be on his way within the next two hours, so you'll get it by this afternoon.

You:	(3) **I'm so happy/glad that you found it/my suitcase. Thank you very/so much.**
Ms Miller:	We are very sorry for causing so much trouble with your luggage. Enjoy your holiday!

2. Words and structures

Choose the correct options and fill in the gaps.

Hinweis: *Für jede richtige Antwort gibt es einen Punkt. Achte darauf, dass du das Wort auch richtig in die Lücke schreibst, da auch die richtige Lösung nicht gewertet wird, wenn sie einen Rechtschreibfehler enthält.*

Turn off your TV

A new study reveals that watching less television may lead to a longer life.
Sitting in front of the television may **be** relaxing. However, spending too **much** time in front of the TV may shorten your life. That's **what** Australian researchers found out. They collected TV viewing information from more than 11,000 people older **than** 25 years. They discovered that people who watched an average of six hours **of** TV a day lived an average 4.8 years less than those who didn't watch any television. They also found out that every hour that participants watched after the age of 25 was associated with a 22-minute reduction in **their** life expectancy.
It's no **mystery** that sitting in front of the TV isn't healthy. If you don't **get** enough exercise, you will probably develop diseases such as heart problems. The lead author of the study states that **watching** TV also lowers life expectancy because of the poor diet that junk-food advertising can promote. He says that it might make sense for doctors to start asking their **patients** about how much time they spend in front of the TV.

Adapted from: http://www.timeforkids.com/news/turn-your-tv/11981 (last accessed on 16.02.2017)

D Text Production

Hinweis: *Achte darauf, nur* <u>*eine*</u> *der beiden Aufgaben zu bearbeiten. Wähle die Aufgabe, zu der dir am meisten einfällt. Gehe auf alle Punkte ein, die angegeben sind. Orientiere dich dabei an der vorgegebenen Wortanzahl. Die folgenden Lösungen sind Beispiele.*

The best thing about your home town

In my home town there is a fantastic leisure park with all kinds of attractions. You just buy a ticket and can stay in the park the whole day.

There is a big roller-coaster, a free fall tower and a ghost train, and also pony rides and a merry-go-round for little children. And best of all: There is an indoor swimming pool with a long slide.
Whenever there is a birthday party, we visit this place because it's fun for everybody. At the weekend many people visit our town to enjoy our leisure park.

Write a text about the picture

In the picture, there is a little boy of about five or six years. He's wearing a white T-shirt with something printed on it. His mouth and eyes are wide open. He is looking very concentrated and excited at the same time because he's holding onto an ice cream cone with eleven scoops on top. It looks like a tower.
The boy wants to keep this "tower" in his hands as long as possible, of course. But in a moment the tower will topple, and the ice cream will melt on the grass.

Abschlussprüfungen an Hauptschulen in Hessen 2019
Englisch

A Listening Comprehension

1. Message on an answering machine
Fill in the missing information.

Hinweis: *Vervollständige die Sätze jeweils mit dem richtigen Wort aus dem Hörtext. Achte darauf, dass deine Lösung verständlich und sinngemäß richtig ist, da du nur dann einen Punkt bekommst.*

Veronica missed her **train**.
She arrives in Liverpool at **8:15** pm.
She will go straight to the **restaurant**.

2. Conversations
Tick (✓) the right statement. There is only one possible answer per statement.

Hinweis: *Du bekommst für jede richtige Antwort einen Punkt. Wenn du mehr als eine Antwort ankreuzt, bekommst du keinen Punkt, auch wenn die richtige Antwort dabei wäre.*

Text 1: At the restaurant

(1) The mozzarella balls are
- ☐ only for Veronica.
- ☐ only for Dale.
- ☑ for Veronica and Dale.

(2) Dale can't have _______ this evening
- ☐ the chicken breast.
- ☑ the steak pie.
- ☐ fish and chips.

(3) They do not want wine because
- ☐ Dale doesn't feel like it.
- ☐ Veronica has to drive.
- ☑ Veronica has a busy day tomorrow.

(4) Veronica needs a new
- ☐ glass.
- ☐ fork.
- ☑ knife.

Text 2: Conversation in the restaurant

(1) At work today, Veronica
- ☐ talked to her boss at ten o'clock.
- ☐ booked flights for her team.
- ☑ prepared the presentation.

(2) Veronica will be away from
- ☐ Tuesday to Wednesday.
- ☑ Wednesday to Monday.
- ☐ Monday to Tuesday.

(3) For her trip, she needs
- ☐ warm clothes only.
- ☐ light clothes only.
- ☑ warm and light clothes.

(4) Veronica has extra work because
- ☐ she had to read her e-mails.
- ☑ a colleague is ill.
- ☐ she left the office early.

3. Survey
Listen to these people talking about embarrassing or annoying parents. Who says what? Write the correct letters in the chart. Be careful – there is one statement more than you need.

Hinweis: *Hier bekommst du für jede richtige Zuordnung einen Punkt. Beachte, dass eine Aussage zu keiner Person passt.*

Roman	David	Christian	Beth	Jenna	Leroy	Tess
H	**E**	**A**	**C**	**B**	**G**	**F**

4. Phone call
Fill in the missing information.

Hinweis: *Hier musst du die richtigen Lösungen in ein Reservierungsformular einfügen. Beachte, dass Rechtschreibfehler zwar nicht gewertet werden, deine Lösungen aber sinngemäß richtig und verständlich sein müssen, damit du einen Punkt bekommst. Der buchstabierte Name muss jedoch richtig notiert werden.*

Circus Restaurant
– Reservation form –

date:	**(the) 29th (of) August / 29 August**
time:	**8/eight (pm) / 8 o'clock (in the evening)**
number of people:	**7/seven**
occasion:	**(dad's/father's) birthday (party)**
last name:	**Cunningham**
phone number:	**01293 784 829**
entertainment:	**magic show / clown / fire eater**

B Reading Comprehension

1. National park rangers

a) **Match the six correct headings to each part of the text (1–6). Be careful – there is one heading more than you need.**

Hinweis: *Für jede richtige Zuordnung bekommst du einen Punkt. Beachte, dass eine Überschrift zu keinem Abschnitt passt.*

part of the text	1	2	3	4	5	6
heading	**D**	**G**	**B**	**E**	**C**	**A**

b) **Answer the questions below. Give short answers.**

Hinweis: *Achte bei deinen Antworten darauf, dass sie verständlich sind, auch wenn Rechtschreib- und Grammatikfehler nicht gewertet werden. Du musst nicht unbedingt in ganzen Sätzen antworten. Deine Antworten kannst du direkt aus dem Text nehmen.*

Why does Ann compare Grand Canyon National Park to a museum?
It shows some of America's most beautiful and historic places.

How do children feel when they look at the canyon?
(They are) amazed (at the canyon's size and colors). /
They think it looks like a painting.

Name one detail of a park ranger's uniform.
- **flat hat /**
- **hiking boots /**
- **National Park Service symbol /**
- **uniform shirt**

What do rangers always carry in their backpacks? (two details)
- **radio /**
- **first-aid kit /**
- **water /**
- **snacks /**
- **sunscreen**

How should a park ranger behave in a dangerous situation?
stay calm (in an emergency)/be prepared (for any situation)

2. Festivals around the world

a) **The following words have more than one meaning. Which of the meanings is the one used in the text? Tick (✓) the correct German meaning. There is only one possible answer.**

once (line 8): ☑ sobald
pour (line 28): ☑ schütten

Write down the German meaning as used in the text.

Hinweis: *Überlege, was das jeweilige Wort im Satzzusammenhang bedeutet, um eine sinngemäß richtige Antwort zu geben. Auch muss sie verständlich sein, obwohl Rechtschreib- und Grammatikfehler nicht gewertet werden. Verwendest du in deiner Antwort die falsche Wortart, bekommst du keinen Punkt.*

honour (line 10): **ehren**

release (line 16): **schwimmen lassen/(Boote) zu Wasser lassen**

season (line 18): **Saison/Zeit**

attracts (line 22): **zieht an/lockt an**

match (line 37): **passen (zu)/entsprechen**

b) **Fill in the correct places. Write down only <u>one</u> place per box. Be careful – there is one tip more than you need.**

Hinweis: *Beachte, dass ein Ort nicht zugeordnet werden kann.*

Where do people	colour each other?	**India**
	celebrate Caribbean traditions?	**London**
	celebrate the lives of the deceased?	**Mexico**
	play and make a mess with drinks?	**Haro**
	enjoy some jokes?	**Montreal**
	have "vegetable-battles"?	**Buñol**

C Use of Language

1. Mediation

a) **Say it in German.**

Hinweis: *In der folgenden Mediation musst du auf Deutsch antworten. Es wird nicht von dir verlangt, vollständige Sätze zu schreiben. Achte jedoch darauf, dass deine Antworten verständlich und sinngemäß richtig sind.*

Sag mir doch bitte zuerst, wie hoch dieser *Mount Washington* überhaupt ist.
1917 m / Meter

Wow! Da hat man ja sicher eine tolle Aussicht. Was kann man denn vom Gipfel aus sehen?
(den) White Mountain National Forest / Vermont / New York / (den) Atlantischen Ozean / Atlantik

Das klingt großartig. Und was kann man dort oben machen?
historische Gebäude besichtigen /
(im Besucherzentrum) Geschenke kaufen /
in die Cafeteria (und auf die Toilette) gehen /
ins „Extreme Mount Washington Museum"/in ein Museum gehen /
Fotos (von der Gipfelmarkierung) machen

Dann lass uns mal nachschauen, wie wir dort hinaufkommen … Ich sehe, dass man selbst fahren kann. Wie lange dauert das?
30/dreißig Minuten

Das ist schneller als ich dachte! Wie sind denn die Straßen dort?
sehr schmal / eng und steil

Oje, ich weiß nicht, ob ich mich dabei wohlfühlen werde … Sag mir doch mal, was in der geführten Tour inbegriffen ist. (3 Informationen)

- **die Fahrt (zum und vom Gipfel)**
- **Informationen durch die Fahrerin/den Fahrer**
- **60 Minuten Aufenthalt auf dem Gipfel**

Das klingt gut, aber es ist sehr schade, dass die Zeit begrenzt ist. Da hat man auf dem Gipfel ja kaum Zeit. Was kostet denn ein Ticket für Erwachsene?
36 $/Dollar

OK. Dein Bruder möchte ja gerne mit dem Fahrrad auf den Gipfel fahren. Was steht darüber auf der Website?
Fahrräder sind auf dem Gipfel (leider) nicht erlaubt.

Alles klar. Dann müssen wir jetzt nur noch festlegen, wann wir diesen Ausflug machen werden …

b) **Say it in English.**

Hinweis: *Lies dir die Aufgabenstellung und die Situationen 1 und 2 genau durch, denn nur für eine verständliche und sinngemäß richtige Antwort bekommst du einen Punkt. Bei Rechtschreibfehlern werden dir keine Punkte abgezogen. Ist deine Lösung aufgrund von Grammatikfehlern nicht mehr verständlich, wird sie jedoch nicht gewertet. Beachte auch, dass du dich höflich ausdrückst, sonst kann dir ein halber Punkt abgezogen werden.*

Situation 1:

You:	(1) **Hello. Excuse me, could/can you help me please? I've/I have left/forgotten my backpack on the bus.**
Woman:	Hi. Yes, of course. That's annoying. But don't worry. Usually other passengers will hand in lost items to the driver. You can collect them at our Lost Property Office tomorrow.
You	(2) **I'm happy/glad to hear that./Oh, wonderful! Can you give/tell me the address, please?/Can you tell me where it is, please?**
Woman:	You will find the Lost Property Office at 200 Baker Street. Good luck!
You:	Thank you very much. Bye.

Situation 2:

Employee:	Good morning. How can I help you?
You:	(1) **Good morning. I would like to ask if someone (has) handed in/turned in a backpack?**

Employee:	Well, let me check. There are a few back here. Can you describe yours, please?
You:	(2) **It's/It is blue with black straps.**
Employee:	Yes, there's a blue backpack here. To make sure it's yours, could you tell me what's inside, please?
You:	Yes, of course. (3) **(There is) a guidebook and a small umbrella (in it).**
Employee:	OK. I found it all. I guess it's yours. You just need to fill in this form and I'll be glad to give it to you.
You:	Thank you very much. Bye.

2. Words and structures

Choose the correct options and fill in the gaps.

Hinweis: *Achte hier darauf, dass du die Wörter richtig in die jeweilige Lücke schreibst! Auch wenn du die korrekte Lösung gewählt hast, wird sie nicht gewertet, wenn sie einen Rechtschreibfehler enthält.*

Gorilla born at National Zoo

On Sunday, the National Zoo in Washington welcomed a baby Western Lowland Gorilla.
The zoo announced **that** this was the first gorilla birth at the zoo in nine years. Mother Calaya cares for her son, Moke, in the Great Ape House.
Moke is the **first** baby gorilla for 15-year-old mom Calaya and dad Baraka. Zookeepers have **observed** Calaya feeding the infant.
They are optimistic that Moke will do well in her care. They have given Calaya motherhood lessons **with** a stuffed toy gorilla.
"We will help her if she needs it, but I am sure that Calaya will be a great mom to Moke," animal keeper Melba Brown says.
Moke will grow up in the **zoo's** gorilla group. In addition to his parents, there are also a young female and an adult female in this group. Two other male gorillas also live **there**. Last Monday, the zoo **closed** the Great Ape House in order to give mother and son some time on their own.
The organisation IUCN has the Western Lowland Gorillas **on** the list of endangered animals. Their **numbers** have fallen in the **past** 25 years because of hunting and diseases in Africa.

Adapted from: https://www.washingtonpost.com/lifestyle/kidspost/western-lowland-gorilla-born-at-national-zoo/2018/04/16/24226d16-41a1-11e8-bba2-0976a82b05a2_story.html?utm_term=.06a4ed795a3f (abgerufen am 13.05.2018, adaptiert

D Text Production

***Hinweis**: Achte darauf, in der Prüfung nur eine der beiden Aufgaben zu bearbeiten. Wähle die Aufgabe, zu der dir am meisten einfällt. Gehe auf alle Punkte ein, die angegeben sind. Orientiere dich dabei an der vorgegebenen Wortanzahl. Die folgenden Lösungen sind Beispiele.*

Superhero

My superhero is my best friend Lisa. She is two years older than me and she has deep blue eyes that sparkle like stars. Her special power is to make me feel better when I have problems with my parents or my friends. She always has a solution and just makes me laugh. When I am ill she comes to see me and tells me wonderful stories. I can trust in her more than in anybody else so I don't know what I would do without her.

Write a text about the picture

***Hinweis**: Sieh dir das Foto genau an. Wer ist darauf zu erkennen? Beschreibe, was die Personen machen, an welchem Ort sie sich befinden und warum sie dort sind. Vergiss am Schluss nicht zu schreiben, was wohl als nächstes passieren wird.*

In the picture I see a woman, a boy and a girl sleeping on a bench at an airport. Maybe it is a grandmother with her grandchildren waiting for their flight. The boy is lying on the woman's legs and the girl is leaning against a suitcase. They are very exhausted because they arrived at the airport early in the morning. Their flight to Turkey was cancelled and they don't know when the next one will go.
Suddenly, they are woken by an announcement: their flight is ready for boarding! They are so happy that they can continue their journey.

Abschlussprüfungen an Hauptschulen in Hessen 2020
Englisch

A Listening Comprehension

1. Message on an answering machine
Fill in the missing information.

Hinweis: Hier musst du die Sätze jeweils mit dem richtigen Wort/den richtigen Wörtern aus dem Hörtext vervollständigen. Beachte, dass deine Lösung verständlich und sinngemäß richtig sein muss, denn nur dann bekommst du einen Punkt.

Tony Morelli is the owner of Tony's **garage**.
He is calling about **(an) application / (a) work experience (placement) / a placement**.
Harry can start working next **Monday**.

2. Conversations
Tick (✓) the right statement. There is only one possible answer per statement.

Hinweis: Für jede richtige Antwort bekommst du hier einen Punkt. Wenn du jedoch mehr als eine Antwort ankreuzt, erhältst du keinen Punkt, auch wenn die richtige Antwort dabei wäre.

Text 1: At the youth hostel

(1) The two friends have booked a room for
- ☐ four days.
- ☑ seven days.
- ☐ nine days.

(2) A hostel card will
- ☐ be cheaper.
- ☐ cost £ 35.
- ☑ save them 10 %.

(3) At the youth hostel they will have
- ☐ breakfast and lunch.
- ☐ lunch plus a hot evening meal.
- ☑ breakfast and an evening meal.

(4) Markus and Andreas do not want to eat
- [ ] regular food.
- [ ] flow calorie food.
- [x] vegetarian food.

Text 2: Making plans

(1) They should start the sightseeing tour with
- [ ] Tower Bridge.
- [x] Buckingham Palace.
- [ ] Madame Tussauds.

(2) The friends are not interested in
- [ ] Tower Bridge.
- [ ] Victoria Station.
- [x] Madame Tussauds.

(3) There is a direct connection to Big Ben by
- [ ] tram.
- [ ] taxi.
- [x] tube.

(4) In the end they decide to
- [ ] go by coach.
- [ ] visit the London Eye.
- [x] use bicycles.

3. Survey
Listen to these people talking about summer holidays. Who says what? Write the correct letters in the chart.
Be careful – there is one statement more than you need.

Hinweis: *Für jede richtige Zuordnung bekommst du einen Punkt. Eine Aussage passt dabei zu keiner Person.*

Mrs Smith	Peter	Mr Gear	Sandra	Alice	Mrs Hall	George
B	**D**	**A**	**C**	**F**	**H**	**G**

4. Phone call
Fill in the missing information.

Hinweis: *Die richtigen Lösungen trägst du hier in ein Reservierungsformular ein. Zwar werden Rechtschreibfehler nicht gewertet, deine Lösungen müssen aber sinngemäß richtig und verständlich sein, damit du einen Punkt bekommst. Der buchstabierte Name muss jedoch auf jeden Fall korrekt notiert werden.*

Davies Court Hostel
– reservation form –

date:	**29(th) September / September 29**
room type:	**single (room)**
number of nights:	**5 / five**
last name:	**Gonzalez**
nationality:	**American**
phone number:	**001 202 555 0124**
special request:	**(reserve a) space for bike / bicycle garage**

B Reading Comprehension

1. Pocahontas

a) **Match the six correct headings to each part of the text (1–6). Be careful – there is one heading more than you need.**

Hinweis: *Du bekommst für jede richtige Zuordnung einen Punkt. Beachte, dass eine Überschrift zu keinem Abschnitt passt.*

part of the text	1	2	3	4	5	6
heading	**C**	**F**	**E**	**A**	**G**	**D**

b) **Answer the questions below. Give short answers.**

Hinweis: *Achte bei deinen Antworten darauf, dass sie verständlich sind, auch wenn Rechtschreib- und Grammatikfehler nicht gewertet werden. Du musst nicht unbedingt in ganzen Sätzen antworten und du kannst die Wörter direkt aus dem Text nehmen. Du bekommst pro Antwort einen Punkt. Wenn du nur zum Teil richtig geantwortet hast, werden keine halben Punkte vergeben.*

When was Pocahontas born?
(around the year) 1595

What did Pocahontas learn as a child?
to make a fire / to cook / to search for food (like berries and nuts)

How old was Pocahontas when the English arrived?
12 / twelve (years old)

Why did Pocahontas want to stay with the English?
She fell in love (with John Rolfe / an Englishman).

What did Pocahontas do in London?
dress in fancy clothes / go to parties / meet King James / meet John Smith

Why did Pocahontas die?
She became (very) sick.

Why do people admire Pocahontas today?
(because) she connected two (very) different cultures

2. Your digital footprint

a) **The following words have more than one meaning. Which of the meanings is the one used in the text? Tick (✓) the correct German meaning. There is only one possible answer.**

hard (line 16): ☑ schwer
mean (line 29): ☑ bedeuten

Write down the German meaning as used in the text.

Hinweis: *Überlege, was das jeweilige Wort im Satzzusammenhang bedeutet, um eine sinngemäß richtige Antwort zu geben. Auch muss sie verständlich sein, obwohl Rechtschreib- und Grammatikfehler nicht gewertet werden. Verwendest du in deiner Antwort die falsche Wortart, bekommst du keinen Punkt.*

content (line 10): **Inhalt**

letters (line 13): **Buchstaben**

way (line 24): **Weg / Möglichkeit / Art und Weise**

raise (line 25): **beschaffen / aufbringen / sammeln**

skill (line 26): **Fertigkeit / Fähigkeit**

b) **Fill in the correct tips. Write down only <u>one</u> tip per box. Be careful – there is one tip more than you need.**

Hinweis: *Beachte, dass ein Tipp nicht zugeordnet werden kann.*

Which tip tells you to	think about what you post?	**4**
	help others?	**5**
	search for your name?	**1**
	delete old accounts?	**6**
	check your privacy settings?	**2**

C Use of Language

1. Mediation

a) **Say it in German.**

Hinweis: *Hier musst du deine Antworten auf Deutsch geben. Auch wenn von dir nicht verlangt wird, vollständige Sätze zu schreiben, solltest du darauf achten, dass deine Antworten verständlich und sinngemäß richtig sind.*

Wir wollen ja im Londoner East End eine Stadtführung machen. Dieses Angebot scheint eine Kombination aus Essen und Besichtigungen zu sein. Welche Sehenswürdigkeiten bekommt man zu sehen? (2 Informationen)

- **(einmalige) Architektur /**
- **historische Stätten /**
- **(alte) römische Friedhöfe /**
- **alte Häuser /**
- **(versteckte) Synagogen /**
- **Street Art/Straßenkunst**

OK, dann geht es also nicht nur um Essen. Wie bewegt man sich da fort?
(Man ist) zu Fuß (unterwegs.) / Man läuft.

Und wer macht dort die Führung?
(unterhaltsame) Einheimische

Wie lange dauert diese Tour?
vier/4 Stunden

Wie viel muss ein Erwachsener bezahlen?
80 Pfund/£

Ganz schön teuer. Wie viele Kostproben sind da inbegriffen?
sieben/7 (Kostproben)

Nenne mir doch mal ein paar Speisen, damit ich weiß, ob das Essen nach unserem Geschmack ist. (2 Informationen)
- **Gebäck/Backwaren /**
- **(englischer) Käse /**
- **Dessert/Nachspeise /**
- **salziges Karamelltörtchen**

Klingt lecker. Was wird denn über die Gruppengröße gesagt?
Es sind nur kleine Gruppen.

OK. An welchen Tagen und Uhrzeiten starten die Touren?
immer Montag bis Samstag morgens um 10 Uhr

b) **Say it in English.**

Hinweis: *Lies die Aufgabenstellung und die Situationen 1 und 2 genau durch, da du nur für eine verständliche und sinngemäß richtige Antwort einen Punkt bekommst. Bei Rechtschreibfehlern werden dir keine Punkte abgezogen. Ist deine Lösung aufgrund von Grammatikfehlern nicht mehr verständlich, wird sie jedoch nicht gewertet. Beachte auch, dass du dich höflich ausdrückst, andernfalls wird dir ein halber Punkt abgezogen.*

Situation 1:

Trudy:	Now this is your room. We'll leave at around 9 o'clock, so remember to get up in time. Do you want me to give you an alarm clock?
You:	(1) **No, thank you. I use my mobile phone as an alarm clock.**
Trudy:	OK. What would you like to eat for breakfast?
You:	(2) **I'm not hungry in the mornings, so I would just like some juice, please.**
Trudy:	I understand – it's the same with me! We'll have a little picnic at the lake. You can eat later.

Situation 2:

Trudy:	What's the matter? Don't you feel well?
You:	(1) **No, I've got a headache and I feel sick.**
Trudy:	Oh dear – poor you. Is there anything I can do to help?
You:	(2) **No, thank you. I just need some rest.**
Trudy:	Yes, of course!

You:	(3) **May/Could I lie down/rest in the car for a while, please?**
Trudy:	Sure, take your time and I hope you'll feel better soon!

2. Words and structures

Choose the correct options and fill in the gaps.

Hinweis: *Schreibe hier die Wörter richtig in die jeweilige Lücke. Ist die Lösung, auch wenn sie korrekt ist, falsch geschrieben, wird sie nicht gewertet.*

Hedgehogs are becoming popular pets

More and more people have hedgehogs as a pet than ever before. Some people think this is strange because hedgehogs **have** spines. They are famous for their spines, which they have **everywhere** except on their face, legs and bellies. Hedgehogs need them to protect themselves while they sleep and when they see enemies. When they are attacked, hedgehogs curl up into a ball. Then **their** spines stand up so that they really feel sharp. Hedgehogs usually sleep in this **position** during the day and wake up to search for food at night. But they are sometimes active during the day too, especially after it **has rained**.

Top on the hedgehog's **menu** are insects, followed by small mice, snails, frogs, eggs and even snakes. Although hedgehogs mostly stay on the ground, they are quite good swimmers and can climb trees too!

People like hedgehogs **because** they are such cute animals. When they are relaxed, their spines feel soft. They have probably become more popular because so many people post lovely photos **of** hedgehogs on social media.

But don't **expect** your pet hedgehog to be like a cat or a dog. You cannot play with hedgehogs. Sometimes you can cuddle with them, but mostly they just eat and sleep.

Hedgehog Facts!, National Geographic Kids, https://www.natgeokids.com/uk/discover/animals/general-animals/hedgehog-facts/; Hedgehog, National Geographic, https://www.nationalgeographic.com/animals/mammals/h/hedgehog/

D Text Production

__Hinweis__: Beachte, dass du in der Prüfung nur eine der beiden Aufgaben bearbeiten sollst. Lies dir beide Aufgaben genau durch und überlege, zu welcher dir am meisten einfällt. Nimm auf alle Punkte Bezug, die angegeben sind. Vergiss auch nicht, die vorgegebene Wortzahl einzuhalten. Die folgenden Lösungen sind Beispiele.

My favourite store

My favourite store is definitely "Bubble" clothes store in Frankfurt, where they always have the latest and most stylish fashion.
For me it's the best store because you can buy unusual clothes there that not everybody wears – and the best thing is that the prices are not too high.
Next week I'm going to buy a pair of designer jeans and a beautiful T-shirt with a special print.
Whenever I go to the store I ask my friends to come with me so that they can also try on and buy the cool clothes there.

Write a text about the picture

__Hinweis__: Hier musst du dir das Foto genau ansehen, um die Details zu erkennen. Gehe auf folgende Fragen ein: Wer ist darauf zu erkennen? Wo könnten die Personen sich befinden? Was machen sie? Vergiss am Schluss auch nicht zu schreiben, was wohl als Nächstes passieren wird.

In the picture there is a man in a suit and a woman in a black dress sitting on a bench with three girls in front of a brick wall. Maybe they are waiting for the bus. They all are holding muffins.
The youngest girl is sitting between the man and the woman. The older girl on the man's other side has a tray with various muffins on her lap. Maybe she offered some to the others before. The man is opening his mouth, trying to take a bite of the other girl's muffin. They are all having so much fun watching this scene that they are going to miss their bus!

A Listening Comprehension

1. Voice mail message
Fill in the missing information.

Hinweis: *Für jede Antwort, die verständlich und sinngemäß richtig ist, bekommst du einen Punkt. Bei der Angabe der Uhrzeit können mehrere Schreibweisen richtig sein. Rechtschreib- und Grammatikfehler führen nicht zu Punktabzug.*

Hal is Paul's **cousin**.
Hal is arriving at the airport at **half past three / 3:30 / three thirty / 15:30**.
Paul must make himself a **sandwich** for lunch.

2. Conversations
Tick (✓) the right statement. There is only one possible answer per statement.

Hinweis: *Für jede richtige Antwort bekommst du hier einen Punkt. Kreuze dabei aber nicht mehrere Antworten an, sonst erhältst du null Punkte, auch wenn die richtige Antwort dabei ist.*

Text 1: Preparing for Hal's visit

(1) Hal
- ☐ has brown hair and blue eyes.
- ☐ has brown hair and wears glasses.
- ☑ is tall and has blond hair.

(2) Hal is staying with Paul and his family for
- ☐ one week.
- ☑ ten days.
- ☐ two weeks.

(3) During Hal's stay, they will
- ☑ go walking in the country.
- ☐ move to Manchester.
- ☐ go swimming in town.

(4) Hal will sleep
- [ ] at Gran's house.
- [ ] in Paul's room.
- [x] in Susie's room.

Text 2: Meeting Hal

(1) On the flight to England,
- [ ] Hal watched three films.
- [ ] a baby screamed for the whole flight.
- [x] Hal wore headphones and fell asleep.

(2) On the day Hal left New York, it was
- [ ] rainy.
- [x] sunny.
- [ ] snowy.

(3) Trifle is
- [x] made with cream.
- [ ] Mum's speciality.
- [ ] an American dessert.

(4) Toad-in-the-hole
- [ ] is made with real toads.
- [ ] is a pudding cooked in the oven.
- [x] is a dish with sausages.

3. Survey

Listen to these people talking about simple ways of saving the planet. Who says what? Write the correct letters in the chart. Be careful – there is one statement more than you need.

Hinweis: *Für jede richtige Zuordnung erhältst du einen Punkt. Eine Aussage kann dabei keiner Person zugeordnet werden.*

Cindy	Rachel	Philip	Harry	Vicki	Kim	Carmen
D	**A**	**H**	**E**	**F**	**B**	**G**

4. Emergency phone call
Fill in the missing information.

Hinweis: *Achte darauf, dass deine Lösung verständlich und sinngemäß richtig ist. Bei Rechtschreib- und Grammatikfehlern bekommst du keinen Punktabzug, es muss aber noch erkennbar sein, was du gemeint hast. Wenn allerdings ein Wort im Hörtext buchstabiert wird und du es falsch notierst, gibt es keine Punkte.*

Warwick Ambulance Service
Emergency details

street:	**Wedgnock Street**
extra detail about location:	**bus stop in front of house**
phone number:	**07911 8870359**
injury:	**(granddad has) broken (his) leg**
how it happened:	**(he) fell off a ladder**
patient's age:	**71**
instructions:	**Don't move (your) granddad/him.**

B Reading Comprehension

1. Nelson Mandela

a) **Match the six correct headings to each part of the text (1–6). Be careful – there is one heading more than you need.**

Hinweis: *Für jede richtige Zuordnung erhältst du einen Punkt. Eine Überschrift kann dabei keinem Textabschnitt zugeordnet werden.*

part of the text	1	2	3	4	5	6
heading	**E**	**B**	**G**	**F**	**C**	**A**

b) **Answer the questions below. Give short answers.**

Hinweis: *Für jede Antwort, die sinngemäß richtig ist, bekommst du einen Punkt. Auch wenn du nicht in ganzen Sätzen antworten musst, solltest du auf Rechtschreibung und Grammatik achten, damit deine Lösung verständlich ist.*

What was Nelson's name as a young boy?
Rolihlahla

Which advantages did white people have during apartheid? Name two.
(they …)
controlled the country /
(had) better lives /
(had) good jobs /
(had) nice homes /
(could go to) good schools /
(could go to) good hospitals /
(could) vote in elections

What was the aim of the ANC?
equal rights for blacks

When was Mandela arrested for the first time?
in 1956

Why did Mandela and the president win the Nobel Peace Prize?
they ended / worked to end apartheid

Where can people read about Mandela's life?
in his book / in *Long Walk to Freedom*

2. Valentine traditions around the world

a) **The following words have more than one meaning. Which of the meanings is the one used in the text? Tick (✓) the correct German meaning. There is only one possible answer.**

patterns (line 22): ☑ Muster
afford (line 28): ☑ sich etwas leisten

Write down the German meaning as used in the text.

Hinweis: *Bei Rechtschreibfehlern wird dir auch hier kein Punkt abgezogen – wählst du jedoch die falsche Wortart, erhältst du keinen Punkt.*

add (line 2): **hinzufügen/dazuschreiben**

kinds (line 7): **Sorten/Arten**

express (line 11): **ausdrücken/zeigen**

carve (line 22): **schnitzen/einritzen**

benefit (line 25): **profitieren (von)/ einen Nutzen ziehen (aus) /einen Vorteil haben**

b) **Fill in the correct countries. Write down only <u>one</u> country per box. Be careful – there is one country more than you need.**

Hinweis: *Beachte, dass ein Land nicht zugeordnet werden kann.*

Which country celebrates	with mass weddings?	**Philippines**
	by giving cutlery?	**Wales**
	by presenting two kinds of chocolate?	**Japan**
	by writing anonymous cards?	**Denmark**
	with a carnival?	**Brazil**

C Use of Language

1. Mediation

a) **Say it in German.**

Hinweis: *Hier musst du nicht unbedingt vollständige Sätze schreiben. Auch gibt es keinen Punktabzug, sofern man versteht, was gemeint ist und die Aussage dem Text sinngemäß entspricht. Beachte, dass du hier auf Deutsch antworten musst.*

Charly ist geimpft, entwurmt und gechippt. Das sind sicherlich Voraussetzungen für die Einreise. Welche offiziellen Anforderungen gibt es noch?
Er braucht einen Tierpass.

OK. Falls wir mit dem Auto fahren, würden wir die Fähre nutzen. Wo verbringt Charly die Überfahrt?
im Hundehotel (auf der Fähre)

Ich weiß nicht, ob Charly seekrank werden könnte. Was können wir vorbeugend tun?
- **Wir sollten vorher mal (auf einem Gewässer) testen, ob er seekrank wird. /**
- **Falls er seekrank wird, sollen wir den Tierarzt kontaktieren, der dann ein Medikament verschreiben kann.**

Alles klar. Grundsätzlich ist er an lange Autofahrten in seiner Box gewöhnt. Welche weiteren Tipps in Bezug auf Hunde im Auto bietet die Website?
Man sollte seinen Hund nicht alleine im Auto lassen.

Eigentlich würden wir ja nur mit dem Auto fahren, weil ich gehört habe, dass Hunde im Flugzeug im Frachtraum fliegen müssen. Schau mal auf der Seite, ob das für alle Hunde zutrifft oder welche Ausnahmen es gibt.
Kleine Hunde oder Assistenzhunde müssen nicht im Frachtraum fliegen.

Ah, OK! Dann würde das doch klappen. Wenn überhaupt, würden wir mit Ryanair fliegen. Da steht doch etwas zu Ryanair. Was ist zu beachten?
Ryanair nimmt keine Hunde mit.

Dann spreche ich nochmal mit deinem Vater. Vor Ort werden wir bestimmt oft U-Bahn fahren. Was kostet ein Hundeticket?
Man braucht keines – Hunde können kostenlos fahren.

Und welche Regeln gibt es sonst noch für das U-Bahn-Fahren?
(2 Informationen)
- **Die Besitzer*innen müssen ihre Hunde immer unter Kontrolle haben. /**
- **Die Hunde müssen angeleint sein … /**
- **oder in einer Box transportiert werden. /**
- **Es muss ausreichend Platz für sie vorhanden sein. /**
- **Sie dürfen keine Gefahr darstellen.**

b) **Say it in English.**

Hinweis: *Lies dir die Situationen, die auf Deutsch beschrieben sind, zuerst genau durch und vervollständige dann die Dialoge. Überlege, wie du angemessen auf Englisch reagieren könntest. Bei Rechtschreib- oder Grammatikfehlern bekommst du keinen Punkt, wenn deine Antwort nicht mehr verständlich ist. Sollte die Aussage trotz Fehlern noch erkennbar sein, wird ein halber Punkt abgezogen. Falls die Höflichkeitsfloskeln („Please", etc.) fehlen, wird für die ganze Aufgabe ein halber Punkt abgezogen.*

Situation 1:

Harry:	Are you all set? The taxi will be here soon.
You:	(1) **Can/May I weigh my suitcase, please? I hope it's 23 kg or less.**
Harry:	Sure, here you are. Let's see … it's 25 kg. What now?
You:	(2) **(I think) I'll put some of my things in my backpack/ rucksack.**

Situation 2:

You:	(1) **May/Can/Could I put my suitcase in the boot?**
Taxi driver:	Of course. Where can I take you?

You:	(2) **To the airport, please. I would like to get out at Entrance B, please.**
Taxi driver:	Yes, no problem.
Taxi driver:	Here we are. That's £18.50, please.
You:	(3) **Thank you. Just keep the change.**
Taxi driver:	Thanks. Have a nice flight!

2. Words and structures

Choose the correct options and fill in the gaps.

Hinweis: *Bei dieser Aufgabe kommt es auch auf die Rechtschreibung an. Du bekommst nur dann einen Punkt, wenn du die korrekte Lösung ausgewählt und das Wort richtig in die Lücke geschrieben hast.*

A profile of Superman

Superman is known as the first superhero in the history of comics. Joe Shuster and Jerry Siegel created him in the USA in the 1930s. At first, Superman was a bold bad person. After a time, he **became** a fighter against evil and for mankind. Superman became more and more popular with readers and so the authors decided to make Superman the **main** figure in the series.

In the story, his father, Jo-El, **sends** him to Earth from the planet Krypton in a small spacecraft. The Kents, a married **couple**, find him and bring him up as their own son. They give him the name Clark and live together in Smallville, Kansas.

As a young man, he discovers his superpowers. For example, he is faster **than** a bullet and more powerful than a locomotive.

Clark also **doesn't** get hurt. He can freeze things and **people**. His best skill is that he can fly. Clark uses **his** superpowers only against criminals and to help humans.

When his father dies, he **moves** to Metropolis. There he works as a reporter **at** the daily newspaper "Daily Planet". Clark pretends to be a shy and clumsy person. He **falls** in love with his colleague Lois Lane. But she only likes the brave and powerful Superman. She does not realize that Clark and Superman are the same person.

http://www.ninthart.com/superman-the-comic.htm (abgerufen am 10. 05. 2020, adaptiert,
https://www.britannica.com/topic/Superman-fictional-character (abgerufen am 10. 05. 2020, adaptiert),
https://www.liveabout.com/profile-of-superman-p2-804272 (abgerufen am 10. 05. 2020, adaptiert)

D Text Production

***Hinweis**: Beachte, dass du in der Prüfung nur eine der beiden Aufgaben bearbeiten sollst. Lies dir beide aufmerksam durch und überlege, zu welcher dir am meisten einfällt. Vergiss nicht, auf alle Punkte Bezug zu nehmen, die angegeben sind. Halte auch die vorgegebene Wortzahl ungefähr ein. Die folgenden Lösungen sind Beispiele.*

A new school club

A cooking club would be great! Whenever I see a cooking show on TV I want to learn how to cook. In a cooking club, both boys and girls could be taught how to prepare fresh, healthy meals for not much money. The teacher should be experienced in cooking and should love teaching it to other people. I think a club like that would be important for pupils because they would learn how to prepare tasty meals themselves and therefore eat less fast food, which would be better for their health.

Write a text about the picture

***Hinweis**: Gehe auf folgende Fragen ein: Wer ist auf dem Foto zu erkennen? Wo befinden sich die Personen und was machen sie? Überlege dir auch, was wohl als Nächstes passieren wird.*

In the picture, there is a park or forest in autumn where a woman and a girl, maybe mother and daughter, are playing football. The girl is trying to kick the ball, but her mother, who is behind her, also wants to get the ball. The girl is stretching out her left arm to keep her balance. Mother and daughter seem to be having a lot of fun. Finally, the girl manages to kick the ball high into the air, and it ends up in a tree. Now, mother and daughter have to find a way to get the ball back down …

Abschlussprüfungen an Hauptschulen in Hessen 2022
Englisch

A Listening Comprehension

1. Voice mail message
Fill in the missing information.

Hinweis: *Setze hier jeweils die richtige Lösung ein. Bei Rechtschreibfehlern bekommst du keinen Punktabzug, wenn die richtige Lösung noch erkennbar ist. Halbe Punkte gibt es bei dieser Aufgabe nicht.*

Callum is calling about the **(football) match**.
It is on **Friday** at eight o'clock in the evening.
Callum will meet Jim at the train station at **5:10/five ten/ten past five**.

2. Conversations
Tick (✓) the right statement. There is only one possible answer per statement.

Hinweis: *Beachte, dass pro Aufgabe nur eine Lösung angekreuzt werden darf, wählst du mehr als eine aus, bekommst du keinen Punkt.*

Text 1: On the train

(1) If Chelsea Football Club win the game tonight, they will be in _____ in the league.
- [x] first place
- [ ] second place
- [ ] third place

(2) Callum bought the two football tickets for
- [ ] £ 65.
- [ ] £ 70.
- [x] £ 130.

(3) The boys go to the Portobello Road Market because
- [x] Caffè Nero will not be open.
- [ ] they would like an American pizza.
- [ ] Callum was ill the last time he had street food.

(4) To get to Notting Hill Gate, they will first take

- [ ] the Central Line.
- [x] the Victoria Line.
- [ ] the Piccadilly Line.

Text 2: At the market

(1) Callum orders the dish of the day because

- [x] it's vegetarian.
- [ ] it's with chicken.
- [ ] he likes fish.

(2) The glasses are

- [x] next to the fridge.
- [ ] behind the serviettes.
- [ ] with the knives and forks.

(3) Jim thinks he left his phone

- [ ] on the train.
- [ ] at a restaurant.
- [x] at the Indian food stand.

(4) The boys decide to get to the football stadium by

- [x] taxi.
- [ ] bus.
- [ ] train.

3. Survey

Listen to these people talking about YouTubers. Who says what? Write the correct letters in the chart.
Be careful – there is one statement more than you need.

Hinweis: *Für jede richtige Zuordnung bekommst du einen Punkt.*

Tyler	Sandra	Julianne	Andrea	Kurt	Maxima	David
E	**A**	**D**	**C**	**F**	**H**	**G**

4. **Phone call**
Fill in the missing information.

Hinweis: *Für jede sinngemäß richtige Antwort erhältst du einen Punkt. Bei Rechtschreib- und Grammatikfehlern bekommst du keinen Punktabzug, wenn die richtige Antwort noch zu erkennen ist – allerdings muss das Wort, das im Hörtext buchstabiert wird, ganz korrekt wiedergegeben werden, damit du hier einen Punkt bekommst. Auch bei dieser Aufgabe gibt es keine halben Punkte.*

VICTORIA HOTEL
– reservations –

from (date):	**August 4th / 4(th) August / 4/8**
number of nights:	**ten / 10**
room type:	**single**
room price:	**£ 87**
last name:	**Vukotic**
contact number:	**07309 558893**
special request:	**(She wants to) bring (her) dog.**

B Reading Comprehension

1. Popular Thanksgiving traditions

a) **Match the six correct headings to each part of the text (1–6). Be careful – there is one heading more than you need.**

Hinweis: *Für jede richtige Zuordnung bekommst du einen Punkt.*

part of the text	1	2	3	4	5	6
heading	**E**	**F**	**G**	**D**	**A**	**B**

b) **Answer the questions below. Give short answers.**

Hinweis: *Hier sollst du selbst die richtige Lösung formulieren. Dabei musst du nicht unbedingt in vollständigen Sätzen antworten, oft reichen auch Stichpunkte. Achte jedoch darauf, dass deine Antworten verständlich sind. Für jede richtige Antwort bekommst du einen Punkt, halbe Punkte werden nicht vergeben.*

When was the first Thanksgiving?
(in) 1621

Why is turkey a popular choice for Thanksgiving today?
(They are) cheap/easy to keep.

How many people participate in the Buffalo "Turkey Trot"?
(about) 14,000

How many people attend the parade in New York?
(over) 3.5 million

Why is there a second turkey now used for the presentation ceremony?
It's a back-up (turkey). / In case something goes wrong.

Name one of the football teams which played in the first Thanksgiving game.
(University of) Yale / (University of) Princeton

2. Seven tips for teenagers

a) **The following words have more than one meaning. Which of the meanings is the one used in the text? Tick (✓) the correct German meaning. There is only one possible answer.**

Hinweis: *Achte darauf, dass du auch hier nur eine Lösung auswählen darfst. Andernfalls bekommst du keinen Punkt.*

say (line 2): ☑ Mitspracherecht
reach (line 7): ☑ erreichen

Write down the German meaning as used in the text.

Hinweis: *Beachte, dass die deutsche Bedeutung des jeweiligen Wortes der Bedeutung im englischen Satz entsprechen muss. Achte auch darauf, die richtige Wortart anzugeben, sonst bekommst du keinen Punkt.*

lead (line 6): **führen**

goals (line 7): **Ziele**

treasure (line 13): **(wert-)schätzen**

know (line 19): **kennen**

around (line 25): **herum/umher**

b) **Fill in the correct tips. Write down only <u>one</u> tip per box.**
Be careful – there is one tip more than you need.

Hinweis: *Beachte, dass immer nur ein Tipp passt, wobei ein Tipp nicht zugeordnet werden kann.*

Which tip tells you	that cool is just a matter of opinion?	**4**
	to just let it happen?	**1**
	that saying no is fine?	**5**
	to remember that friends will come and go?	**3**
	to accept it when something goes wrong?	**2**
	to seek help when things get too much?	**7**

C Use of Language

1. Mediation

a) **Say it in German.**

Hinweis: *Hier musst du die nötigen Informationen aus dem englischen Text („Brighton – family day trip tips") nehmen und auf Deutsch wiedergeben (für Antworten auf Englisch gibt es keine Punkte). Es reicht dabei, wenn du in Stichworten antwortest. Achte aber darauf, dass deine Aussagen richtig und verständlich sind.*

Brighton ist doch an der Südküste! Wie lange dauert die Zugfahrt? Am Ende haben wir gar nicht ausreichend Zeit, etwas zu erleben.
weniger als eine/unter einer Stunde

Das ist wirklich nicht lange! Ich möchte auf jeden Fall zuerst zu dem neuen Aussichtsturm. Wie hoch fährt man da eigentlich?
138 m

Das ist sicher nicht ganz billig. Wie viel kostet es denn für einen Erwachsenen?
16,50 £

Das ist viel Geld! Aber es lohnt sich sicher. Was kann man denn alles von dort oben sehen? (2 Informationen)
- **Brighton /**
- **die Landschaft /**
- **die Küste/Küstenlinie**

Das hört sich gut an! Und danach an den Strand! Es ist ja kein Sandstrand, also können wir keine Sandburg bauen. Was können wir denn stattdessen am Strand machen?
schwimmen (gehen) /
Muschelschalen/Steine/Strandglas sammeln /
auf der Promenade spazieren gehen /
bunte Strandhütten/Stände mit Meeresfrüchten/Läden mit Kunsthandwerk entdecken

Und falls es regnet, dann können wir Minigolf spielen. Das soll ungewöhnlich sein. Was ist denn dort so besonders?
Man spielt im Dunkeln und es leuchtet alles (z. B. Dinosaurier oder tropische Tiere).

Wunderbar! Wir müssen dann auf jeden Fall noch den berühmten Pier besuchen. Was gibt es dort alles? (2 Informationen)
- **ein Fish und Chips-Restaurant /**
- **Stände mit Essen und Trinken /**
- **eine Achterbahn**

Dort können wir bestimmt auch diesen „Brighton Rock" finden, von dem ich gelesen habe. Was ist das eigentlich?
eine Zuckerstange (mit Minzgeschmack) / eine Süßigkeit (aus Zucker)

Na, das klingt doch super! Lass uns gleich mal nach Zugverbindungen schauen.

b) **Say it in English.**

Hinweis: *Lies dir beide Situationen genau durch, damit du verstehst, wie du auf Englisch antworten bzw. welche Fragen du stellen musst. Achte darauf, dass deine Lösungen verständlich sind, sonst bekommst du einen Punktabzug. Ein halber Punkt wird dir abgezogen, wenn du die Höflichkeitsfloskeln vergisst.*

Situation 1:

You:	(1) **Excuse me, please, can we walk to Madame Tussauds from here?**
Passer-by:	You could do that, but it's a long way.
You:	Oh, OK. (2) **What is the best way to get there?**
Passer-by:	Actually, you can take the bus or the underground. But I would say the underground is your best option at this time of the day.

You:	OK, I understand. (3) **Where is the nearest underground station, please?**
Passer-by:	That would be Tower Hill right over there.
You:	OK, thank you very much.
Passer-by:	No problem. Enjoy your visit, bye.

Situation 2:

Assistant:	Hello, how can I help you?
You:	(1) **We'd like/We would like to go to Madame Tussauds.**
Assistant:	OK, I see. Then you want to take the Circle Line. It will take you straight to Baker Street.
You:	(2) **Thank you! How far is Madame Tussauds from the station?**
Assistant:	It's just up the road, not too far.
You:	Great, thank you.
Assistant:	You're welcome – bye.

2. Words and structures

Read the text, then tick (✓) the correct words.

Hinweis: *Wähle hier das richtige Wort im Satzzusammenhang. Für die korrekte Lösung bekommst du jeweils einen Punkt.*

From a postman to a TikTok star

"There once was a ship that put to sea" is the first line of a famous old sea shanty. It is called *The Wellerman*. While working on board their ships, sailors sang sea shanties. The lyrics of *The Wellerman* are (1) **about** whaling. It was an important but dangerous work for sailors hundreds of years ago.

This old song became popular again during the Covid-19 pandemic. (2) **It** was a successful online hit all around the world for months. The sea shanty also (3) **changed** the life of 26-year-old Nathan Evans from Scotland. Nathan worked as a postman in his hometown in Airdrie. He only enjoyed singing in his free time. In 2020, Nathan, who also writes songs, uploaded his (4) **performances** to different social media accounts.

Then (5) **his** nephew and niece wanted him to try out TikTok. They said to him, "There's this thing, it's called TikTok, and you need to get on it." But he thought that it was only about kids dancing, and that was not the place where he wanted to be. In the end, Nathan (6) **gave in** and created an account. So, in July 2020, his musical career started.

(7) **Since** January 2021, his life has been a whirlwind. The clip *The Wellerman* (8) **reached** Number 1 in the UK, in Germany, Austria and Switzerland. It also stayed at the top of the charts for ten or more weeks. Nathan gave up his job (9)

as a postman to concentrate on his music career. He told the BBC, "It's crazy and has gone much further than I ever thought it (10) **would** go."

https://www.theguardian.com/music/2021/jan/16/how-a-scottish-posties-simple-sea-shanty-struck-a-global-chord, https://www.bbc.com/news/uk-scotland-glasgow-west-55661351, https://www.bbc.co.uk/programmes/articles/3rP00S1tTw2j2shv6TWtwHl/sea-shanty-star-nathan-evans-i-thought-tiktok-was- for-kids (alle abgerufen am 15.07.2021, adaptiert)

D Text Production

Hinweis: Beachte, dass du in der Prüfung nur eine der drei Aufgaben bearbeiten sollst. Lies dir alle Aufgaben genau durch und überlege, zu welcher dir am meisten einfällt. Nimm bei der Bearbeitung auf alle Punkte Bezug, die angegeben sind. Halte auch ungefähr die vorgegebene Wortzahl ein. Die folgenden Lösungen sind Beispiele.

Who has the most delicious food?

I'm going to bring a traditional potato salad from my home region. You make it like this: cut the boiled potatoes into thin slices, season them with salt and pepper, then add hot broth, oil and vinegar. If you like, improve your salad with slices of pickled gherkins and onions. As the salad doesn't contain any meat, I can also recommend it to my vegetarian classmates, and the non-vegetarians can eat it with German sausages. My Indian classmate is going to bring a spicy curry – I'm sure it will be my favourite!

Write a text about the picture

Hinweis: Gehe auf folgende Fragen ein: Wer ist auf dem Foto zu sehen? Wo befinden sich die Personen? Was machen sie? Du sollst dir auch überlegen, was wohl als Nächstes passiert.

A man, a woman and a girl are standing in front of some English terraced houses with two cars parked in front of them. The man is standing on the pavement with his arms wide open and a book in his hand. He is looking at the girl and seems to be asking her: "Don't you recognise me?" as the girl looks a bit unsure. The woman, maybe her mother, has put her arm round the girl's shoulder and is explaining to her who the man is. Now the girl remembers him – it's her uncle who she hasn't seen for many years.

Write a text about the picture

***Hinweis**: Beschreibe in deinem Text, wer auf dem Foto zu erkennen ist, wo sich die Personen befinden und was sie machen. Überlege dir auch, was wohl als Nächstes passieren wird.*

In the picture, some boys are trying to show tricks on their bikes in a street with skyscrapers, maybe in New York. The boy in front of the picture is standing with one foot on the bike saddle whereas his other leg is stretched out sideways. He seems to be very good at it. Another boy at the back of the picture is riding his bike on the rear wheel and is also doing it quite well.

The boy in the front, however, will lose his balance a moment later and tip over his bike. Luckily, he won't hurt himself.

Abschlussprüfungen an Hauptschulen in Hessen 2023
Englisch

Um dir die Lösungen zur Prüfung 2023 schnellstmöglich zur Verfügung stellen zu können, bringen wir sie in digitaler Form heraus.

Sobald die Original-Prüfungsaufgaben 2023 freigegeben sind, können die dazugehörigen Lösungen als PDF auf der Plattform **MyStark** heruntergeladen werden. Deinen persönlichen Zugangscode findest du auf der Umschlaginnenseite vorne im Buch.

Aktuelle Prüfung

www.stark-verlag.de/mystark

PRÜFUNGS-
ANGST

STOPP DIE PANIK

Mit der Fußsohlen-Methode

Prüfungen können Angst- und Fluchtsituationen sein. Dein Körper schüttet Adrenalin aus und dämpft das Gefühl in den Füßen. Z. B. beim Weglaufen ist es gut, wenn man die Füße nicht spürt. Eine Prüfung ist aber **keine Gefahrensituation**. Signalisiere deinem Körper, dass du nicht weglaufen musst, und bring das Gefühl in deine Füße zurück:

Setze oder stelle dich hin.
Die Füße müssen den **Boden** berühren.

Schließe jetzt deine Augen und **denke** dich in deine Füße hinein.

Fahre in Gedanken um die **Fersen**.

Spüre den **Druck** auf dem Boden.

Erkunde den **Bogen** deines Fußes.

spüre jeden einzelnen **Zeh** von klein bis groß.

Dein Körper **fühlt** die Füße wieder und denkt,
er sei in keiner Panik-Situation, sondern in **Sicherheit**.

www.stark-verlag.de **STARK**